ETCHED IN DARKNESS

VEIL OF SHADOWS

BOOK SEVEN

M. R. PRITCHARD

Paperback ISBN: 978-1-957709-47-5

About Veil of Shadows

"Veil of Shadows" delivers a riveting blend of Supernatural & Constantine with the pulse-pounding tension of The Walking Dead, unveiling an unrelenting battle between good and evil. Delve into a realm of fated mates entwined in a deadly dance, where bad omens are a harbinger of darkness. As lovers turn to foes and friendships are tested, join the struggle against Angels, Demons, and the living dead. Brace yourself for an action-packed, paranormal dark romantic fantasy you won't be able to put down.

———

"Etched in Darkness" is book 7 in the Veil of Shadows Series. You can start here if books 1-6 are not your jam. The next few books in this series will focus on Jed and Shay's relationship and can be read without books 1-6. We will go back in time and revisit old friends. Then catch up with Sparrow and Meg's timeline.

———

If you want to immerse yourself further in the Veil of Shadows, visit the blog for Veil of Shadows discussions, previews, and spoilers.

About Etched in Darkness

When darkness beckons and love defies the unknown, destiny takes an unexpected turn.

Jed is a hybrid on the run, forever hunted by Angels and Demons; he should have never survived. Now that all Hell has erupted on Earth, Jed is making his way to California to explore a supernatural darkness that just might save him.

Shay's college plans are ruined. Thrust into the apocalypse, she thinks she has a strong chance of survival since she was raised by preppers. She's wedged between parents who are trying to shelter her and a trusted ranch hand who's overstepping boundaries.

Paths cross when a search and rescue mission turns to disaster. The charismatic ranch hand makes a deal with a crossroads Demon for Shay, and the family ranch.

The veil between planes is thinning and this just might be the end of Jed's solitary days. Jed can't walk away from the toughest cowgirl he's ever met.

Chapter 1

Running for your life wasn't a sport on the Earthen plane, but for Jed, it was survival. Jed had been on the run since he could walk on two legs and finally escape the creatures that came for him day and night. Since he was Nephilim, this was the way it would always be. He'd been around for a while. He'd been hunted for a while. He knew this from the few others he'd met that were like him. They didn't last long, but they traded stories and methods to stay alive. Jed tapped his pocket, feeling the notebook of spells that was left to him by the last Nephilim he'd come across decades ago. Declan wasn't much older that Jed, but he'd lasted by way of spells and runes carved into every flat surface of his house and belongings. Jed took it one step further and carved those runes into his skin. It was good practice since now he could make a living with the tattoo gun. But, every so often, a creature would walk through the doors of his shop that didn't belong. Like Meg did that one day. Meg, with her dark energy and light eyes. There was something about her he didn't understand. She paid in full and held conversation while he tattooed the watercolor sparrow over her heart. He revealed little about himself. It was when she came back again and brought that fallen-Angel Hellion Sparrow that she wound up ruining the pleasant spot he was at in life. Sparrow was all kinds of cursed. Jed could see it the moment he laid eyes on the guy. Worse was that Meg was head over heels in love. He helped them, tattooed them with runes of protection. And all it got him was noticed.

Jed touched the mark on his neck. He also lost a little blood when Meg bit him. Jed tried to shake away the feelings. Lust and heat had filled his body. He remembered touching her waist before he passed out. Whatever she was, he wanted more but he also wanted to never see her again. Meg was trouble. Trouble he didn't have time for if he wanted to stay alive.

Now here he was on the run again, making his way toward the rural towns of the Midwest, away from the crowded cities of the Northeast. With any hope, he'd avoid the dead until someone else took care of them and he'd avoid Angels and Demons and dead things as well. He'd find food and shelter and hunker down until it was safe again.

Jed stopped under the awning of an empty gas station. The dead hadn't been walking for long, a few months at least, but the destruction and abandon was rapid. Jed glanced through the glass of the gas station and auto shop to see if there was anything inside worth investigating. His pack was heavy with clothes and food, his water jug half-full. He focused on the shelves behind the counter. He could use a smoke. It had been a long time since he set a cancer stick to his lips. He gave up the dirty habit when New York State outlawed them. It surprised him Indiana hadn't outlawed them too.

The sound of shuffling feet broke the afternoon silence. On this daily trek from Walkerton to Kingsbury, Jed hadn't seen much life. He was sure the dead were making their way to nearby Chicago. They always seemed to move with purpose, clustering in small groups. Something drove them to move and follow as one.

A man's voice startled Jed. "A large herd of zombies are making their way through California."

Jed walked to the door of the gas station and found the television mounted in the far corner of the waiting area. A map of the U.S. replaces the reporter's image; the movement of the dead is illustrated with green blobs like weather radar. There's a large area of green over southern California, moving north. They color the area south of the green zone black. A dead zone. A universal warning. Do not go there.

"If you're still in northern California and you're hearing this message, evacuate. Evacuate now! The Coast Guard has abandoned the west coast. The National Guard has declared California a complete loss."

Jed focused on the spattering of green where he was traveling. The Midwest wasn't overly populated, it would be easier to hunker down. His gaze went to the west coast again. The green blob travelled along a main highway. He found that interesting. The dead didn't care about roads, they moved through forests just as haphazardly. It was almost like they were following something.

The news reporter rubbed his face and looked thoroughly terrified. There were loud thuds from the television and a light fell over and hit the desk where the reporter sat. The reporter stood. "Evacuate now!" he shouted one last time before picking up his chair and throwing it. A dead woman walked across the News set before the screen turned to static.

Jed glanced at the shelves and noticed some of the snack foods hadn't been completely pillaged. There was a handful of Slim Jims, Oreos, and a few tins of Spam. Jed went for the protein. The sugary cookies might taste good, but he knew he'd be feeling like crap the next day.

There was a change in the air. Something like mild electricity popping. Turning, he noticed a figure walking down the street.

Jed paused, crouched, and watched the tall man walking down the road. Angel wings were invisible on this plane, but he could see their transparent glimmer. He always knew when they were near; feathered or leathered, he could see the wings in the right light.

This was an Angel. Come to put an end to his life, since he was forbidden and all. They never stopped. Jed traced his footsteps in his mind and tried to think of any clues he could have left behind. He'd been careful on his travels. He was always careful. Never left a trail or a crumb or much of a memory. He was good at being invisible. He was beige in an ochre world, blending in with vacant faces and warm bodies. He tipped his hat lower to hide his face. A shuffling sound echoed.

Jed whispered a spell of glamour and his fingers tapped gently in spellcasting. He leaned to the side and didn't see his reflection in the glass window of the gas station. He scooted forward, careful not to step on any debris that would make the Angel walking down the road notice him. He made his way out the door, keeping to the shadows. He stopped once he got around the corner of the building.

The shuffling sound got louder. It didn't seem to bother the Angel walking down the street. He was tall, lithe with muscle, a blade drawn. His clothing was similar to what most wore on the Earthen plane; leathers and linen or jeans and a T-shirt. A Demon he'd be able to spot based on clothing alone. They were always in full leather. Dark leather, black or deep red like a kidney bean. The Angel gripped his blade and walked with purpose. Jed wiped sweat from his brow, worried the glamour wasn't doing its job.

The wind blew.

Jed sneezed.

Shit.

The Angel picked up his pace and began running in Jed's direction. The shuffling sound got even louder as five of the dead broke onto the street and went after the Angel.

Jed ran. He wasn't a coward; he just knew it was easier to avoid the creatures that came for him than expend the energy needed to kill them. He needed to save his energy for the important battles.

Chapter 2

Shay counted the supplies that lined the root cellar. It was deep underground and cold. She stepped on a hole near the wall, grinding her foot until the soil collapsed inward. Sometimes small animals or bugs dug their way into the cellar. Usually they left empty handed because the food was sealed and packaged to last years. There were root vegetables in bins. Shay opened the lid on one to make sure whatever came through the hole hadn't made a home here. This food needed to last them.

She twisted the lid on the wooden barrel and lifted. The soil covered potatoes looked undisturbed. She closed the lid and rotated the barrel as best she could. There weren't any chew marks or holes. She moved on to the barrel of carrots, another of onion, and lastly the beets. Everything looked undamaged. She swiped at her hair, wishing for a hot shower sometime soon.

"Everything good down here?" a familiar voice asked.

Shay's spine went straight, and her heart picked up a

few beats. "All good," she replied, turning to face the man who'd entered the cellar. It was Clyburn.

Shay took the laminated list out of her pocket and held it out. "Everything's stocked." She sidestepped to avoid him. "I'm headed up to help with dinner."

"Whoa," Clyburn said, holding out his hand. "Where ya going so fast, little lady?"

"I have things to do." She avoided his hand and glanced at the door. The man was obstructing her way out. "I don't have time for this."

He settled his thumbs in the belt loops of his jeans and looked down. "Why you always avoiding me, Shay?" He sounded dejected.

She took a few more steps, wishing he'd move the hell out of her way. "I have to go."

Clyburn took a few steps. He was toying with her.

Shay didn't like the feeling of being trapped. Hated it more and more each day. Hated that Clyburn felt the need to find and harass her. Shay took her chance at the unobstructed passage and ran for the door of the root cellar.

Clyburn was faster, grabbing her around the waist and pulling her back against his chest. He laughed and tightened his arm around her middle.

"Let go of me." Shay struggled, wanting to scream.

Clyburn pressed his cheek against the side of her head. His scruffy beard scratched at her face. Shay could smell the sweet and earthy scent of his chewing tobacco. "Mmm. You smell good," Clyburn said, his voice deep and low.

Shay scrabbled at his arms, hoping to leave marks under the flannel shirt he wore. She wanted him to let go.

"My father is expecting me. He'll be here any minute."

Shay was unsuccessful in stomping his foot since Clyburn wore steel toed boots.

"Maybe I want to invite you to the square dance on Friday."

"Doubt they'll still be having it." Shay didn't stop struggling.

"They will. Going to be a powwow too."

"If we're all still alive by then." She knocked her head against his and saw stars.

Clyburn finally released her. "We'll definitely be alive," he said.

Shay ran out the door and up the uneven steps of the root cellar entrance. She slammed the door closed and ran as far from the cellar as she could.

Shay passed a stockpile of logs, the gardens, the barns where the chickens and pigs and goats stayed. She ran past the houses and the rusted tractors. She ran past the tall Ponderosa Pine that set their property apart and made it easy to find if you got turned around in the beyond. Shay finally stopped at the horse barn. Out of breath, she gripped the wooden stall door. A black stallion wandered over and nuzzled her head.

Shay's heart was beating fast, and she wanted nothing more than to melt to the ground. The stallion could tell she was upset and nuzzled harder against her shoulders.

"You're such a gentleman, Nero." Shay patted the stallion's neck. "More so than anyone else here."

Shay hid in the horse barn until her father came looking for her.

———

"Shay-baby," Nicholas called. "I know you're in here."

Shay heard the enclosure open and looked up from where she was sitting in Nero's corral. Sweet hay crunched under her feet as she stood. Nero whinnied and walked closer. Ready to protect.

"It's okay," Shay said as she reached out and patted Nero on his flank. "It's just dad."

Nicholas took up the doorway to the paddock, a giant man dressed in dusty jeans and a rugged button-up shirt stained with dirt. He tucked a pair of gloves into his pocket and brushed his hands off on his pants. The man was part cowboy, part prepper, and he had been wrapped around Shay's finger since the day she was born.

Shay's father taught her everything she knew: how to grow a garden, how to store food, how to ride a horse, shoot a gun, hunt a bison. Most importantly, he'd taught her how to survive the apocalypse she never thought would come. It came. Headfirst, the apocalypse rammed through their Montana ranch with death and destruction. It had only been a few months, but many had died. They hadn't lost a soul on the ranch and there was enough food and supplies to keep them going for years. But Shay didn't intend to stay holed up on the ranch for years. She'd had plans. They involved seeing the world. She'd been accepted to Brigham Young University in Utah on a scholarship. She wasn't sure where the biological sciences would take her but she knew it was a good starting point. It would've taken her places. But now she was stuck. She'd probably never see the rest of Montana, let alone college in Utah, or anything else. Shay was having a hard time accepting that she was stuck on this ranch, only to be pursued by Clyburn, probably for the rest of her life. She figured she still had plenty of living to do before settling down and couldn't accept the idea of it right now.

"Why are you hiding out in here?" her father asked.

"Nero was lonely. I brought him some carrots." Shay didn't like lying, but she also didn't want to admit that her father's favorite ranch hand had been after her for months now. Clyburn wanted a relationship. Shay wanted nothing to do with the man. He was strong and handsome and capable, but Shay was simply not interested. They were only a few months into the apocalypse. Things could change. The dead could drop and leave humanity alone. If nothing she had hope for something better than their current situation. It couldn't get worse, could it?

"You got a good girl here, Nero," her father laughed as he patted the horse, then brought Shay in for a hug. He kissed the top of her head. "Momma made chicken and dumplings. Come on." He tugged at a piece of hair that had fallen out of her ponytail.

Shay left the horse corral, only feeling safe now that her father was there. They walked out of the barn, the heat of summer cooling as evening came. In the light, Shay noticed blood on her father's boot. She'd seen a lot of blood lately. More gore and brain matter than she ever expected to see in her life. She didn't take pride in it. Slamming a poker through a walking corpse's head to get it off the fence was a necessary evil these days.

"Did they get in?" she asked.

"No." His voice was grim. "There was a lone one walking across the fields. Must've heard the animals. The fence kept it out, but we put an end to it and burned the body." He pointed to black smoke rising in the distance. "Damned soul bought himself a six-foot deep oven to have its last rest in."

"Will they ever stop coming?" Shay asked.

"Never know." He pulled her shoulders against him in a brief hug. "Don't worry, Shay-baby, I'll protect you."

Shay nodded, and Clyburn's actions made more sense now. He'd been high on adrenaline after killing one of the walking dead. He was looking for another rush involving her, of course. Shay needed to carry a concealed weapon. Clyburn thought she was easy prey, but she wasn't. Eventually, she'd have to unleash on him.

CHAPTER 3

JED MADE IT PAST THE OUTLYING CITIES OF Chicago unharmed. He'd hitchhiked through Iowa, surprised that people stopped to give him a ride. He assumed everyone was a little more forgiving now that most were running for their lives on a daily basis. But Jed had that effect on people. They were eager to help him, eager to listen, eager to offer food and drink. He figured it had something to do with him being a Nephilim. Whatever energy he carried, the people of the Earthen plane were willing to assist him. Especially the women. Jed did his best to hide his face with messy hair and a baseball cap pulled low. He could hide with his magic, but his face was easily identifiable and easily remembered. He hid from cameras. Preferred small towns with limited infrastructure. Big brother wouldn't keep his secrets. If a traffic camera caught his image, the Angels and Demons would come soon after. They always did. It was a hard lesson that led Jed to a simpler life.

The Angel was still hunting him. Jed could sense it. He couldn't stay glamoured invisible forever. The spell would drain his reserves. He had to be smart, calculated, careful. His fingers lingered over the fresh spell of protection he'd inked on his skin. It burned and he didn't have a tegaderm to cover it with. First world problems. There was a time when fresh tattoos were never covered. They were left out to weep and crust until the image broke through like an egg hatching.

His back thudded against the rusted metal of the truck bed as it drove over a few potholes. The cab was full. A father named Bill, a young mother named Laura, and two little girls. He took one glance at them and volunteered to ride in the truck bed. The mother sighed in relief after taking in the tattoos covering his arms. The little girls glanced out the window at him every so often. He didn't ask their names, didn't want to know. He didn't want to make connections and remember. He'd learned the hard way.

They stopped at a rest stop near the South Dakota border just past a road sign for *Meckling: Population 2,500.* Bill got out, shotgun in hand. He passed Jed a baseball bat.

"Girls have to use the bathroom," Bill said.

Jed stood and jumped out of the truck bed. He weighed the baseball bat in his hand, liking the feel. He had a few weapons tucked away. Knives that were carved with spells, a small handgun with not nearly enough bullets. Jed preferred a blunt object to swing. The baseball bat was perfect.

They walked toward the rest stop building slowly, taking in their surroundings. Bill skirted across the flowerbeds to get a good look behind the building. It was mostly glass with two doors. If anyone was there, they'd see.

The enclosed bathrooms made Jed's body tense with anticipation. He didn't like killing things, but the walking dead were already... dead. They were just stuck on the wrong plane. Their souls should've gone to Hell for sorting, but something was happening between the realms. Something dark was walking the Earthen plane, disrupting the natural order of things. Hence the apocalypse and the zombies. Jed was trying his best not to get caught up in it, but since Meg was the last to visit him before all Hell broke loose, he figured he was slightly involved already.

Jed gripped the baseball bat as Bill opened the door to the rest stop lobby. They listened. There were no noises. No smells. No grunts or groans or shuffling feet.

Bill pointed to the lights. At least this place still had electricity. It was out most places. But Jed knew the rural areas would still have men and women with purpose, doing their best to hold humanity together as long as they could. He was sure they'd come across some open restaurants, maybe even a hotel with hot water.

Bill motioned to the women's room and Jed walked closer to back him up. Bill pushed open the door, crouching to look under the stalls. As Jed followed behind, Bill walked through the bathroom, using the barrel of his shotgun to push open the stall doors. When he got to the fourth and final one, he turned to Jed with a look of relief.

"All clear?" Jed asked.

"Yup," Bill replied. "Let's check the men's room."

They passed two vending machines filled with snacks and soda. Bill pointed. "We need to empty those before we leave."

"Good idea." Jed pushed open the door to the men's

room. He paused, crouching. There was a set of boots in the last stall. Jed held a finger to his lips and gripped the bat like he was about to hit a home run on the bottom of the ninth.

Bill readied his shotgun.

Jed sidestepped to the last stall and prodded the door with the toe of his boot. "Come out."

There was a noise from inside, a gurgling and a grunt.

Jed kicked the door as hard as he could.

A dead man hissed. His hair was ragged and half fallen out, teeth rotten and putrid.

"I got it," Bill said, moving into place.

The dead man stumbled forward.

Jed hit up with the bat, knocking the dead man in the chest and forcing him to stand up straight.

Bill blew off its head in one shot.

The carcass fell backward onto the toilet and the door closed.

"Watched all those movies about zombies my whole life and I'll still never get over it." Bill shivered. "God save us all."

Jed headed for the door. "You should get the girls."

They'd cleared the building in less than ten minutes. Still, Jed didn't like the idea of leaving Laura and the girls alone in the truck. Surprise was a battle tactic and, as far as Jed was concerned, every moment was an opportunity to die, especially so these days.

Chapter 4

Shay woke to a scratching sound outside her window. She sat up, hurried, rolled out of bed, and grabbed the flashlight from her nightstand as she dropped to the floor. The old farmhouse was two stories but the roof to the covered porch was outside her window. It was easy to access if anyone wanted to. As a teenager, she'd snuck out to watch the stars on the rooftop enough times to know someone was there now.

There was a hunting knife under her mattress. Shay reached for it and sat up just far enough to get a good view of the window and a man-sized shadow.

Shay froze and watched. It took a few moments before she recognized the figure.

Clyburn.

He tugged at the window, trying to open it.

Shay flattened herself to the floor, waiting until the noise stopped and she recognized the sound of him climbing down from the roof.

Shay finally stood and checked the locks on the

window. Thankful she'd remembered to lock them before falling asleep.

Clyburn approached her in the morning, a steaming cup of coffee in one hand and a piece of paper in his other. He walked toward Shay, looking tired, smiling when her eyes didn't look away.

"You dropped this." He held out the root cellar list.

Shay reached for it but Clyburn moved the paper once, twice, three times before she plucked it from his fingers.

"Thanks." Shay tucked the list in her back pocket and stepped down off the front porch.

"Where are you going?" Clyburn asked.

"Wherever I want." Shay headed for the horse barn.

"They're fed already." Clyburn sipped at his coffee.

Shay stopped walking, turned to look through the kitchen window at her mother and father talking as they washed dishes together. She wished her father would walk through that door so Clyburn would go away.

"You should stop avoiding me." Clyburn said. "I'm perfect for you. Your father agrees."

Shay made a face. "Nero is perfect for me. I don't need a man."

Clyburn laughed and kicked at the dirt. "I know the ranch. I can keep you safe." He looked past the fence surrounding their ranch. "I can protect you from what's out there."

"I don't need protecting." Shay said. "And don't try to break into my bedroom window again." Shay tapped the small hunting knife she'd tucked into her cargo pocket of her pants. She wanted to whip it out and stab him in the shoulder. She could do it too, she knew it would only take her about five seconds. Shay took a deep breath. She wasn't the maiming type, at least not yet.

Clyburn crossed his arms, resting his wrist and coffee mug in the crook of his arm. He smiled. "Thought you heard me."

"Be lucky my father didn't. He'd have shot you dead on the spot."

Clyburn stuck out a finger to point at her. "That's where you're wrong. If he kills me, I turn into one of those walking corpses." He snapped his jaw, straight teeth clanking together. "Then I bite, and everyone turns." He leaned closer. "He won't shoot me dead. He wouldn't risk your life. Be happy I'm not some city boy from back east with no sense of survival. Cowgirl up, this is happening."

"Over my dead body." Shay waved. "Nice speakin' atcha." Shay headed for the horse stall, not trusting Clyburn to have actually fed Nero. There were plenty of lies she'd caught him in, which is why she didn't trust the man. She was sure that Nero's stall would have an empty oat bucket and yesterday's water.

Shay was thankful that Clyburn didn't follow. She'd had enough of his nonsense. There was no way in Hell she'd carry on with him. No sense in it. She couldn't believe her father would even consider it.

"You know I won't be living forever." Her father's voice called from the wraparound porch as he stepped down the stairs to follow her.

"Yes, you will, daddy," Shay said. "You're the heartiest survivor I've ever known."

"Why don't you go to the square dance with Clyburn?" he asked.

Shay sighed loudly. "I'm not going. It's not safe."

"We have to have some fun. I'll bring momma. We can double date." He smiled but Shay could tell it was forced.

"I'd rather dye my hair blue." Shay looked up at her father. "Daddy, I don't need a man to take care of me. You taught me everything I need to know to survive. Momma read me all the books. Heck, I reread all the books."

Her father reached out and touched her hair. "This might look nice blue. I just want someone to take care of you."

"I don't need anyone like that. Definitely not a ranch hand." Shay shivered, wishing she'd put on her jacket.

"There aren't many options these days, darlin'."

"We'd have to leave the ranch to know." Shay pointed toward town. "My knight in shining armor could be waiting for me over yonder."

Her father laughed, then coughed. "Maybe we'll go check then."

Shay's brows rose in interest. Her father hadn't let her leave the ranch since the dead walking had spread to Montana. She didn't really want to go anywhere now. She was safe here, but she knew she needed to get out in the real world eventually. She needed to put her skills to use. She needed to… do something else.

———

THERE WERE two other ranch hands; Clyde and James, who stayed on the property. They were old and had no interest in Shay. They simply wanted to survive. James was one-hundred percent Northern Cheyenne Indian and left on the weekends to see his family on the reservation.

Clyde was an old friend of Nicholas' who had gotten into enough trouble throughout his life. He spent most of his time smoking on the porch and watching old movies on the television. Clyde watched the news every day and updated them all. He told Shay's father where the walking corpses were heading, where they'd been, where the National Guard was headed–it was nowhere near Colstrip, Montana.

When Friday came, James was packed and ready to head to the reservation.

"What about the powwow?" Clyburn asked.

"No." James shook his head. "Not a good time." He looked up at the sky. "There are evil spirits nearby."

"Maybe you should stay another day," her father suggested.

James tightened a strap on his horse and patted his saddlebags. "I have to see how they are. I've been here long enough. Telephone lines are out. Cell phone service is down." James pointed to Clyde. "Old man says the television is mostly static, all week long. I have to go." James fitted his foot in a stirrup and launched himself onto the horse's back. "I'll be back Monday." He tipped his hat.

Clyburn opened the front gate and let James go. They all stood and watched him ride the horse across the prairie. A few little birds fluttered out of his way.

James had planned his route during dinner. He was going to stay on the outskirts of Colstrip, head south avoiding route 39, and stick to the valleys between the mountains. He'd travel around Lame Deer, cross US-212 just west of the casino and enter the reservation from there. Nicholas had asked a few questions to verify James's route.

"I've done it plenty of times," James reminded him. "Decades worth."

"The dead didn't walk then," her father reminded James.

Shay had a bad feeling in her stomach. The towns weren't highly populated, but she didn't think James could protect himself if too many of the walking dead came after him. He could go into the mountains and lose them in the rough terrain, but it was risky. There were snakes and elk and bears that wouldn't be afraid to go after him.

CHAPTER 5

Bill and his family were headed to Saskatchewan. He'd told Jed they had more family there, and the Canadians weren't having as much of a crisis as the U.S. They were taking Montana Highway 59 north. Jed needed to take US-212 West.

"Good luck, man," Bill said with a firm handshake.

"You too," Jed said, securing his pack.

"You should stop at one of these stores and get some new gear." Bill pointed to a shop down the road. "No one will care these days."

"Sure will." Jed patted the side of the truck as Bill got behind the wheel. He waved to Laura and the little girls, hoping they wouldn't remember his face.

Jed hit the road walking, thankful that the family had driven him across a few states without getting harmed. The Angel that was tracking him outside Chicago must've lost his trail.

Mountains flanked US-212 on each side. He could see far in the distance. He figured he'd make it to Ashland by nightfall. As he walked, he practiced minor spells. He stretched and exercised his fingers so they'd bend and tap in awkward positions during spellcasting.

One truck drove by him and slammed on the brakes.

Jed saw the man looking in his rearview mirror.

The driver put the red truck in reverse, moved to the middle of the road, and stopped next to Jed.

"Whatcha doin out here?" asked the driver. He was young but missing a few teeth. There was a rifle propped between the seats.

"Just passing through," Jed said.

"Well, you wanna ride?"

Jed didn't really want a ride. He wanted to walk and clear his mind and keep up his stamina. He looked toward the mountain. There was nothing out here. He was more likely to die by wild elk attack out here than zombie bite.

"Sure, man," Jed reached for the passenger door.

"Name's Dan," the driver said. "You?"

"Jed."

"I can drop you in Lame Deer. I'm headed up to Nichols. Unless you want to go that way." Dan hit the windshield wiper button and blood smeared across the windshield. "Sorry about that. Hit one of those walking dead people."

"I'm headed west." Jed adjusted his pack between his feet.

"Welp, Lame Deer has a casino that's still up and running. I can drop you there. I drove by yesterday and it still had the lights on."

"Thanks," Jed said.

Dan drove fast. The speedometer hovered around one-hundred miles per hour. There was nothing else on the road, so Jed didn't complain. He was just happy to be riding shotgun and not in the truck bed.

Jed studied Dan from his periphery. It was odd, the guy showing up out of nowhere. Jed didn't trust. He didn't trust miracles and he didn't trust help that was too good to be true. He couldn't see any wings or horns. He rubbed a rune on his hand, considered casting a spell right here in front of a stranger.

Dan slammed on the brakes. The truck skidded to a stop.

Jed reached for his gun, ready to fight in close quarters. He noticed the bite mark on Dan's arm. Shit.

"Whoa, chill out, pal." Dan pointed across the street. "Casino."

Jed sighed a breath of relief, feeling like an idiot. "Thanks." He said as he opened the door and got out.

Dan took off before Jed could get a good grip on his pack. "Hey! My bag!" Panic flashed through Jed's body. Everything important for staying alive was in that pack. Dan stopped the truck and shoved the pack into the street.

Jed jogged after his belongings as Dan's truck accelerated down the road before turning sharply right.

"Asshole," Jed muttered, picking up his bag. Jed didn't curse him much, Dan wouldn't need it. He'd be dead soon; a walking bag of flesh like the others, lost and wandering the Earthen plane, his soul in unrest. Jed should've killed the guy. He should have prevented Dan from hurting others. God forbid the guy turned while he was driving. He shook his head, knowing better. Can't save them all. Jed knew he could only save himself. This life was meant to be lived alone. Letting someone get close to him meant they would only end up on the run forever or dead. Jed wouldn't do that to another soul.

Jed took in his surroundings. The casino was tiny but offered lodging and food. Jed had been traveling nonstop for weeks. He was ahead of schedule and didn't want to show up in California too early. He headed for the casino.

Chapter 6

James never came back. By Tuesday, Clyburn and Nicholas were packing up the horses to go find him.

"I want to go," Shay said, holding Nero's harness.

"No," Clyburn said first.

"Daddy," Shay stared at her father.

"Who will take care of momma while I'm gone?" her father asked.

"Momma is a strong woman who can take care of herself," Shay said.

"You packed that horse?" her father asked.

"Yes." Shay tipped her chin up. "I got my firearms, extra bullets, hunting knives, water, snacks, and a change of underwear."

Clyburn chuckled.

Shay's eyes threw daggers.

"You might as well let the lady tag along," Clyburn said.

Shay could barely believe it. After all of his jabs about her needing protection, he was going to be on her side in this argument. Maybe he wasn't a total tool. Shay glanced at the bulge in his lip from packed chewing tobacco. Nope. Still a tool.

"Go tell momma goodbye," her father said. "That woman will tan my hide if you leave without kissing her cheek."

Shay ran into the house to speak with her mother before leaving. Then, the horses were trotting through the gate of the ranch and Clyde was locking it behind them.

"Bring James home," Clyde said, as they galloped away.

———

Shay's horse followed her father. Clyburn was a few yards behind them. They traveled parallel to Highway 34 and stopped briefly at Castle Rock Lake for the horses to drink. There were figures wandering around the Colstrip Inn & Suites hotel in the distance. Their clothing looked ragged, their skin pale and sallow, they barely lifted their feet while walking.

"You think they're dead?" Shay asked.

"Most likely," Clyburn replied, studying the lake water as though he could see something beneath the surface.

"They won't come," Nicholas said, patting his horse and leading it away from the lake. "As long as we are quiet."

Shay opened her water and took a drink before following her father.

"Let's get out of here," Clyburn said as he mounted his horse. Shay and her father did the same.

They traveled past the Lake and around the sandy runoff from the abandoned mines.

"There won't be much past here," her father said. "Until we get to Lame Deer."

They followed the path James said he'd take. There were tracks from his horse and his boots, and broken stalks of bramble.

Out here in the valleys of Montana, all seemed normal. There were rabbits and snakes, a chilled breeze blowing in from the west that promised winter would be on its way soon. Shay zipped her jacket.

The squealing of rubber tires on the road and a revving engine broke through their silent trek. "Wait," Nicholas held up his hand.

Shay reigned in Nero. Clyburn stopped his horse next to Shay.

"Don't look good," Nicholas said.

There was a red truck driving erratically. The windshield wipers swiped back and forth across a blood smeared window.

"We should go," Clyburn said.

Shay watched the truck weave all over the road. It accelerated abruptly before turning sharply to the left, hitting a narrow embankment, and rolling.

"Shouldn't we help them?" Shay asked. She knew better than to ask but it was the human thing to do. She'd want someone to help her if someone injured her in a car accident.

"We don't help the damned," her father said. "Let's get out of here before the corpse crawls out and comes after us."

Shay clicked her tongue and Nero picked up speed.

The three travelers rode south at a fast pace. They

didn't see James, but they followed the tracks of his horse until they stopped at US-212. There were no tracks on the opposite side of the pavement.

They rode east, toward Lame Deer center.

"He wouldn't have gone towards town," Clyburn said.

"Right about that," Nicholas said, inspecting the tree line for clues.

"This isn't the route he told us he'd take," Shay reminded the men.

Chapter 7

Jed pushed open the door to Lame Deer casino. It was single story, more of a glorified motel than a hotel. The carpet was emerald green, the walls gold and burgundy. It smelled like cigarette smoke, but underneath there was a stench he couldn't put his finger on, musky and dirty. Something he didn't like lingered.

He walked to the front desk and reserved a room for the night.

"Checkout is at eleven in the morning," the young guy with a goatee said as he searched for the room key.

Jed paid and took the key with the number nine on it. "The sign said there's a buffet." He hadn't eaten a proper meal in days.

The desk guy pointed to the other side of the room. "Closes at nine tonight."

"Thanks." Jed walked through the casino toward the rooms. He opened the door to room nine and threw his bag on the bed. Jed pulled the knife out of his pocket and etched a rune of protection into the doorframe. Jed pulled back the covers on the bed and checked for things normal people would never look for: runes of blood, clasps of hair, piles of ash or sand, hex bags. He found nothing, but left his own mark for safety.

Jed made his way to the buffet after locking his belongings in the room. The casino looked to be about three-quarters full. There were security guards watching everyone closely. They would ask to check arms, wrists, and necks for bite marks. Jed rubbed his neck where Meg had bitten him. Thankfully the scar was small. He adjusted his shirt so the guards wouldn't see.

The buffet wasn't much to write home about. There was overcooked steak, soggy broccoli, and a cheesy pasta dish that had congealed on the serving spoon. He filled his plate with all of it. The food might not be top tier but it was warm. A young woman at the bar offered him a pale lemonade or water. Jed took one of each. He sat near the window in an empty booth and watched out it as he ate. He glanced out the window multiple times to ensure that Angel didn't drop out of the sky to continue his hunt.

The smell of smoke lingered in the dining room along with the musky smell from before. There was something dead here. A rat in the walls, a possum in the ceiling, or a human in a closet somewhere.

Jed finished his meal and walked through the casino. He fished a coin out of his pocket and sat down to play the slots for a few minutes. He won ten dollars. Played it all and lost it. It was a decent way to kill fifteen minutes; made him appear human, just like the rest of the casino guests. Most of the workers had tanned skin and pitch-black hair. If he had to guess, Lone Deer was owned and run by local Native

Americans. He made a mental note to do some research on the area. He went to the lobby for some reading material. There was a shelf with an array of pamphlets. Jed took a handful. He wouldn't be going to any museums or on any recreational day trips to the reservation, but he could read about it before continuing on to California in the morning. Last, he grabbed a map of the west. He already had a path planned out, but he wanted to make sure he wasn't missing anything.

Stomach full and showered clean, Jed relaxed on the bed. He'd pushed a dresser in front of the door, just in case. The bathroom window was big enough for him to crawl out of if needed. There was never a moment he wasn't planning. He was sure it was the only way he'd survived this long: have a defense plan and an escape plan for every moment.

He fell asleep reading about the Northern Cheyenne Indian Reservation.

CHAPTER 8

SHAY WOKE BEFORE THE SUN. NERO WAS NUDGING her. She sat up and inched herself away from Clyburn. He'd snuck too close to her during the night. She smoothed her palm over Nero's cheek.

"Good boy." She patted him and took in their surroundings. They'd stopped to camp just outside of Lame Deer. There was a campsite near the waste station. It smelled just bad enough that no one in their right mind would bother them.

Shay got up and started getting ready for the day. She rolled up her sleeping bag and packed it. She took the horses to wander, eat the sweet grass, and drink from the trickling stream nearby. Nicholas and Clyburn had taken turns staying awake and watching over camp during the night. Nothing had disturbed them, only the chill on the wind.

Nicholas and Clyburn woke and packed up their things.

"We'll head for Lame Deer. Should be there before brunch," Nicholas said.

The crew made their way to the road, grateful that they no longer smelled the waste station fumes. An SUV drove by with two women inside. They looked scared, their faces pale and eyes wide. They didn't stop. The driver gave them a wide berth as she sped by.

"You think something happened here?" Shay asked.

"Probably," Nicholas said.

There was a sound in the trees nearby. A whinny, the clopping of hooves. A horse galloped out of the tree line headed for them. Dappled brown and white, they all recognized the horse.

"That's James's horse." Clyburn reached for the reins and brought him in.

There was blood on the saddle.

"Where'd he go?" Nicholas asked the horse.

Shay knew a bystander might think of them as nuts for asking a horse a question, but horses were smart. They knew things. They loved their humans just as much as humans loved them.

The horse huffed and shook his head toward Lame Deer.

"Show us," Nicholas said as he took the horse's reins and headed toward town.

"Stay close," Clyburn warned.

Shay swallowed the lump that was growing in her throat. Whatever happened to James could not be good. He was rarely without his horse, especially while traveling. They'd gone from the ranch to the reservation hundreds of times over the years.

More cars sped out of Lame Deer. Soon there was a line of cars and trucks leaving, while they were the only ones headed to town. A few beeped their horns and waved, warning them.

"Turn around," they shouted out the window.

The last car simply blessed themselves, forehead, chest, shoulder to shoulder and whispered a prayer as they went by.

———

Lame Deer was a steaming pile of dung. Cars were burning. The Dollar Tree was burning. WinCo foods was burning. James's horse led them straight to the Casino.

"Of course," Clyburn muttered in disgust.

Shay knew James liked to gamble, but she barely believed he'd run off to the casino in the middle of all this.

"None of us are without our faults," Nicholas said, clicking his tongue at the horse.

They all had guns ready but the sounds of screams and crashing directed the attention of the dead elsewhere. Through some miracle, they made it to the casino parking area unscathed.

James's horse huffed and nodded his head toward the casino door.

"We know," Nicholas patted the horse. "We'll go get him."

"Do you think anyone is alive in there?" Shay asked.

"It's not on fire, so I have some hope," Nicholas said. "Stick together."

They tied up the horses under a sprawling oak and headed for the front entrance to the casino.

Chapter 9

Jed woke to the smell of smoke, acrid and unpleasant. He jerked upright and looked at the door. The smell was faint-maybe not coming from the casino?

Jed got out of bed and dressed in a hurry. There were strange noises outside his door; thuds as something heavy knocked against the wall. He hurried to get dressed and shove his belongings into his bag. Tying his boots, he heard faraway screams and shouting. Shit. This couldn't be good. He grabbed the pamphlets off the nightstand and shoved them in his pocket, then moved the dresser away from the door and looked out the peephole. The pale eye of a dead woman looked back.

"Shit," Jed muttered to himself. He reached for the fixed-blade machete knife secured to the side of his bag. It was the best weapon for fighting the living dead. A gun was too loud and brought more. And his magic didn't protect him well from souls that were trapped on the wrong plane. They existed in some strange way. He'd yet to find a spell or rune that would take care of them. Jed looked out the window to get a good idea of what he was up against.

Suddenly, a man in dusty jeans and a button-up shirt was striding down the hall, past the window, and struck the dead woman in the head with a sickening *thwack*.

The man knocked on his door with two pounds of his fist.

Jed opened it and did his best not to look at the brain matter that was dripping down the door.

"Hey. I'm looking for James Crow. Indian looking guy with black hair down to here." The man motioned to his shoulder.

"Not here." Jed adjusted his pack. "How bad is it?" he asked.

"Town is gone. This place will be done for soon." The man moved on and knocked on the door next to Jed's room.

Jed stepped into the hallway. Doors were opening up and plenty of people were still alive. Under the scent of smoke, he smelled breakfast.

Jed made his way to the lobby. Two men were dragging a dead body out the back door. From what he could see, there was already a small pile of bodies. There was no sense of chaos or panic so he turned in his room key.

"What's going on here?" Jed asked the goateed guy at the desk.

The guy moved slowly as he picked up the key and found the hook where it hung until the next guest. "Dead overtook Lame Deer during the night. Most of the town is on fire. We're holding down the fort here." He motioned to the door. "Already had armed guards employed. A few of the dead got in but they took care of them."

"That's good," Jed said.

"Sure you don't want to stay? Few stragglers have come in and said it's terrible out there. You could stay here until it clears up."

"I need to be getting on," Jed said as he tapped the counter. "Thanks though."

Jed went to the dining room. There was bacon, eggs, and French toast. He piled his plate high, not knowing when he'd eat like this again. He grabbed two cups of coffee and sat near a window in the corner. He didn't want any surprises. As he ate, he watched the smoke billow out of the buildings about a half a mile away in the center of town.

He shifted to the side and pulled out the pamphlet with the town map and studied it. Last night he'd planned on walking straight through town. Now he needed to avoid it. US 212 was the quickest route; going south would bring him past more shopping and houses. To the north, there was less in terms of people clustering, but he'd have to trek through a lot of rugged, elevated terrain.

Jed thought of the waterways of the Great Lakes region he'd already traversed. So many times he had to make his way around the little finger lakes and canals. Some elevated terrain would be nothing in comparison. The canopy of trees would hide him from anything flying overhead, hunting him.

Jed ate the eggs first. He added too much salt and pepper, but he didn't care. Seasoned food would be scarce soon enough. The bacon was a little soggy but dipped in syrup tasted just fine. He glanced at the buffet, wondering if it would be selfish to get another plate and two more coffees. He watched the door and tried to get an idea of how many guests were out there. He checked the clock. Since it was nearly ten and only a few tables were occupied and there were mounds of food, he went up to the buffet for more.

Long ago, Jed worked as a line cook in a small diner. It wasn't hard work and he'd learned a lot. Butter is your friend, salt the fries before the grease dried, melt all the cheese with a little steam. The bacon could have been left on the griddle for another two minutes, then it would be crispy. Jed took six slices. They overcooked the eggs. Jed knew the eggs should've been set in the serving pan when they were three-quarters of the way done because they'd continue to cook as they sat. He took four slices of French toast and the two coffees. Returning to his seat, he piled the dirty plates together so the staff wouldn't have to. It was a slight gesture to let them know he wasn't a total heathen.

Voices were shouting in the lobby.

Jed leaned to the side to get a look as he shoved food in his mouth and chewed.

The guy in the button up and dusty jeans was at the lobby desk. The guards were fighting at the door.

Jed ate faster figuring he was going to have to leave soon. He shoveled the eggs into his mouth and considered tucking the French toast into his bag for later. There was a crashing sound, followed by growling: inhuman noises that Jed knew only came from walking corpses. He stood, swallowing a cup of coffee in three gulps. Glancing to the back of the room, he looked for a door that might let him out. There was only a door that led to the kitchen. In the back of the kitchen there'd be a door to the outside, but he wasn't sure he wanted to venture through any rooms he couldn't get a good look at. He didn't want to be a sitting duck. He reached forward and inspected the window where he'd eaten. It didn't open.

Jed headed to the threshold to the lobby, French toast in hand. He took a bite as he walked, wishing he had slathered it in butter before leaving.

The lobby had a front door that was currently under siege. The opposite side of the lobby had a patio with seating and a growing pile of bodies. Directly across from him was the casino floor with guests still playing the slots and cards as though the apocalypse wasn't taking place around them. The man in the dusty jeans was asking the goateed guy behind the desk about someone named James. He motioned with his hands, explaining James's height, hair, and complexion. The guy with the goatee nodded and pointed to the patio.

The dusty jeans guy slapped a hand over his mouth. There was another guy with a wad of chewing tobacco punching out his lower lip and a girl that appeared to be with him. They all showed signs of disappointment. If he had to guess, James was dead and was one of the bodies in the pile on the patio.

Three things happened in the next moment. The glass to the front lobby shattered. The girl turned, drawing her gun and taking the stance of a cowgirl ready to shoot. And Jed got a good look at her, which made him drop his French toast.

CHAPTER 10

Somehow, all the dead in Lame Deer were trying to come through the door of the casino. Shay was ready. She had enough bullets to take out some of the dead. Nicholas was backing up to protect her. Clyburn was closing in on her right.

The door strained under the weight of the horde pushing against it.

"James is dead," Nicholas said over his shoulder. "We need to get out of here. Fast."

"Gotta go now," Clyburn said. "Those doors are going to shatter soon."

The three moved as one, backing toward the patio behind them.

Movement caught Shay's eye and she glanced to her left. A man stood in the doorway, dropping his food on the floor as their gazes met.

Shay's breath hitched. She'd seen plenty of men come through these parts but she'd never seen a man covered in strange tattoos or so tall or... striking. There was no other way to describe him. He tried to hide it with a low base-ball cap and messy hair, but Shay saw him. She felt her face flush as she stumbled. Her father stepped on the toe of her boot. Clyburn grabbed her arm to stop her from falling.

Glass shattered and burst across the room. Red dripped into her eye.

"Damnit," Nicholas spat. "Run."

Gunfire erupted as security began taking out the dead filtering in through the front doors.

They ran. Clyburn shoved the patio door open. Shay and Nicholas ran through before turning to secure it.

"Don't trap them," Shay said, rubbing blood off her forehead and out of her eye.

Clyburn was pushing a heavy table in front of the door when it burst open. Metal slammed against metal and Clyburn skirted out of the way.

It was the guy with the tattoos.

Nicholas slapped Shay on the back and pointed to the area where they'd tied up the horses. It was a clear shot.

"Go," Clyburn said as he ran across the patio to clear the way.

Shay ran, focused on Nero in the distance. The horses stayed quiet and she was thankful for that. The noise brought the dead and Shay hoped they didn't lose their focus on the front doors of the casino.

Nicholas got to the horses first and untied their reins. Shay shoved her foot into the stirrup and launched herself onto the saddle with everything she had. Nicholas and Clyburn did the same.

"Around the foothills," Nicholas said, pointing. "There

won't be any of the dead wandering through there for a while."

"Hee-yaw," Clyburn took off to scout the trail.

Nicholas held the reins of James's horse as they escaped the casino grounds.

Shay turned to get one last glance at the casino. Smoke rose from the front of the building. The guy with the tattoos was walking across the patio, digging a piece of paper out of his pocket. He saw her, indecision plastered across his face. He looked like a hitchhiker with his travel pack and worn boots.

"Here," Nicholas had a piece of cloth in his hand. "For the cut." He motioned to her forehead.

Shay took the cloth and pressed it to her skin. In the excitement, she hadn't felt the glass shards cut her face, but now she did. A sharp ache stretched from her hairline to just above her left ear. Momma was going to lose it when she saw the cut. Shay tried to get a good feel for the edges and the deepness of the wound. With all the blood, she was sure she'd need stitches.

Shay focused on Clyburn's back as he made sure the trail ahead was clear. Maybe the ranch hand would back off now that she was mutilated. Men rarely lowered their standards.

Shay gripped Nero's reins tighter and squeezed her legs together to gain some balance. It was hard galloping with one hand to her head. Shay could smell the acrid smoke from Lame Deer burning. She could smell the iron tang of blood running down her face. Her stomach lurched. Nero could tell something wasn't right and slowed his galloping.

"Come on," Nicholas said.

Clyburn turned when he heard Nicholas's voice. He turned his horse, galloping fast and rounding Shay. "Cowboy up," Clyburn urged. "Should've stayed home like your daddy said."

"Shut your hole." Shay's mouth felt dry, her tongue heavy.

"Did ya get bit?" Clyburn asked, suddenly worried.

Shay's mind raced. Had she been bit? They came across a few of the living dead but her father and Clyburn had cut off their heads. Shay didn't touch a soul. She kept her distance. The only thing was her cut face. Shay swallowed down the lump in her throat. What if the broken glass cut the dead before cutting her? What if their disease was a pathogenic type? They only knew it spread by being bit but what did anybody actually know for certain these days? It could spread by body fluids. If that was the case, Shay had little time left. She only hoped she'd be home in time to tell her momma goodbye.

Nero picked up his pace, the motion jerking Shay. Her head throbbed and blood began dripping into her eye again. She pressed the rag against her cut. Her vision blurred, she swallowed down the urge to vomit, and then, everything went black.

CHAPTER 11

Jed was sure he didn't want to get around Lame Deer by heading south, but he was on the heels of locals. They had to know better than him how to avoid the onslaught in the center of town. He picked up his pace, focusing on the cloud of rising dust ahead of him. He wasn't sure he'd be able to keep up with a horse's gallop. The crashing sounds coming from the casino prompted Jed to get moving. He took to following the horse tracks at a fast pace. Every few hundred yards, he'd take to the elevated foothills and hide his shadow among the pine and fir trees. He hadn't forgotten about that lone Angel who was searching for him near Chicago. Usually when one got near, they didn't stop tracking him.

The locals led him into the depths of the Montana wilderness. He remembered the pamphlets he'd looked at the night before and figured they were on the edge of the reservation grounds. He could still hear the screams and tire squeals from Lame Deer and the casino siege. Jed glanced behind himself every few hundred yards. The dead didn't hurry. At least he had that. They were easy to outrun. It was the quiet ones that showed up like a jump scare from behind a closed door or a run down car he worried about. Out here it shouldn't be a problem. He was far enough from town he'd only have to worry about a safe place to sleep or... the locals on horseback in front of him. If one of them went, the game plan would need to change.

Jed thought of the girl at the casino. He tried not to, but one glance had made him drop the precious French toast. Jed would like to meet her again, even if second encounters were dangerous. He relieved himself near a Douglas fir, wishing he'd grabbed a bottle of water before leaving the casino. There were spells to bring water if need be.

Jed walked along the ledge of the foothills. The pace of the group traveling slowed and he could no longer see their cloud of dust. He wondered if something had happened. The surrounding forest became thicker, the trees close together and harder to walk under. Jed descended the hill and walk along the hoofprints. He grabbed onto a skinny tree trunk, noticing an odd bend in it. Nearly a ninety-degree angle. He let go and ran down to the trail below. He walked for a bit, slowing when he felt a prickle on the back of his neck.

Shit.

Jed reached for his knife, but a quiet whoop distracted his attention. Suddenly, a man was standing in front of him. Tanned with hair black as pitch, the man didn't look happy.

"You're on the wrong land," the man said.

Jed's hand moved slowly to grip the knife in his pocket.

"Sorry, man. Didn't know there was a difference in land here. Thought it was all God's land."

The man scowled. "You don't belong here. Your kind doesn't belong."

Jed was confused. This wasn't an Angel; he wasn't a Demon. The dark-haired man in front of him whistled. Eight more men moved out of the surrounding tree cover.

Jed began whispering the words of a spell, his fingertips tapped against each other lightly.

"No!" one man shouted, throwing a handful of dirt in Jed's face.

A mouthful of dirt was enough to impair his spell. He'd hoped to go invisible and escape, but as he coughed on the Montana dirt, he couldn't get the words out correctly. There was nowhere to run.

Jed looked up. If he had wings he could fly out of there, but he'd never been born with them and he'd only ever seen one Nephilim with some that were mutated and too small.

He didn't get to plan for an escape much longer, because someone smacked him in the back of the head and it was lights out.

———

Jed woke to his arms and legs tied together. His back ached and felt raw, like they had dragged him. Panic set in as he realized his bag was missing and his pockets were empty. Jed rolled to sit up and took in his surroundings. Eyes bleary and gritty, it took him a minute or two to focus in the darkness. There was noise outside and the crackle of a roaring fire. Deep voices were arguing. Jed was in a room with one door, one window, a lamp with no shade and a slowly dying bulb. He noticed his gear on a table near the door. This was not how he wanted his travels to go. He needed to get the heck out of here. Jed struggled against the ropes on his wrists and ankles. He figured he must've upset the natives when he wandered onto the reservation. These people definitely had something against him. He'd never come across this problem before.

Jed whispered the words of a spell and flexed his fingers. The ropes at his wrists and ankles dropped away like falling paper. He flexed and stretched the stiffness out of his arms and legs. Now he needed an escape plan.

Chapter 12

Shay's head was pounding. The steady humming of deep snoring made it worse. She recognized the sweet smell of chewing tobacco. Clyburn was nearby. Too close for comfort. She felt a knee pressing into the back of her thigh and inched away. She tumbled onto the floor. Catching herself on a hand and shoulder, Shay groaned.

How the Hell did he get into bed with her? Shay rubbed her face, stopping when she got to the bandage across her forehead and ear. Her skin ached and burned. She tried to scowl and felt the pulling of stitches. Shay moved to stand, weary on her feet. She tried to remember what had happened before getting here. The furniture was familiar. She'd been here before. They were on the Reservation. Probably at the family of James Crow. Damn. Shay didn't envy her father for having to break the news to the Crow family that James was dead.

If they were on the Reservation, then they had gone in the complete opposite direction of home.

Shay made her way to the door, eager to put distance

between herself and Clyburn. Eager to let loose on her father about Clyburn invading her space much too often. Shay thought she'd made herself clear when she told Nicholas she didn't need a man like Clyburn to protect her. Fear settled in Shay's belly. If Clyburn was this close, was there something wrong with her father? Shay opened the door and strode down the long hallway that led to the center of the Crow family home.

She stopped in the kitchen, gripping the back of a chair at the breakfast nook to steady herself.

"You shouldn't be moving so fast," a familiar voice said. It was Grandmother Crow. "Sit now. I'll bring you something to drink."

Shay's head was spinning, and she didn't think she'd be able to stand much longer. She rounded the chair and sat.

The old woman set a steaming mug in front of her.

"Is my father okay?" Shay asked as she wrapped her hands around the mug and let it warm her fingertips.

"He's fine. Out with the men, working on a plan to get you home." The old woman fussed with the bandages on Shay's forehead. "I'll give you a salve so it doesn't scar too badly."

Shay flexed her forehead, feeling the pull of the stitches.

"Don't." The old woman smacked Shay's shoulder. "You'll stretch the skin and the scar will hold. Don't move your face until it's healed."

"I'm assuming that will take weeks." Shay brought the mug to her lips. "I can't move my face for weeks?"

"I did the stitches myself. Don't ruin my hard work." Grandmother Crow went back to her cooking.

The front door opened, letting in brisk morning air.

Shay shivered. Summer was coming to an end quickly and being at the Reservation meant the ride home would take two nights by horseback. They could take Forks Rd to Highway 4 by truck, but that would lead them back to the center of Lame Deer.

Nicholas walked through the door with the other men of the Crow family.

"We should bury him on our lands," a tall man with a beaded tail of hair said.

"We can show you where we found him," Nicholas said. "Not sure how much of him will be left after the dead are done."

Crap. Shay didn't expect her daddy to sign up to go back to Lame Deer. If they hadn't run so fast, they could've brought back James's body. She didn't like the idea of going back to the casino.

"You're upright," Nicholas said, focusing on Shay. He walked closer, inspecting her face. "You gave us quite the scare with fainting and falling off Nero." He touched the side of her head. "Clyburn carried you all the way here."

Shay scowled at the thought of Clyburn touching her for more than a mere second. The tugging of skin and side eye from Grandmother Crow forced her face into a placid expression.

"Don't be like that, Shay-baby," her father said. "You were out for a while. Wasn't sure what to do before the Crow boys came along." Nicholas thumbed toward the crew of men getting comfortable in the living room.

Shay could remember four of their names: Elsu, Hosa, Iye, and Jacy. She always wondered how James got such a different name from the other men in his family. But he was the only one who left the reservation to find work. Maybe he had another name she never knew about.

Iye waved to Nicholas to join their meeting. He patted Shay's arm before leaving the kitchen nook where she sat.

Shay sipped at her tea and listened to the men. Her father told the others what they'd endured in Lame Deer. Elsu laid a map on the coffee table and the men discussed a path. The Crow men had a good idea of clusters of walking corpses in Lame Deer. They talked about traveling Forks Rd via trucks until the Pow Wow Memorial on Highway 4. There were some trails along the valleys of the foothills, but they'd have to approach the casino from the south.

"Might be able to sneak onto the property and get James without those walking dead noticing." Jacy rubbed his neck as his eyes studied the map.

"What about that Allegewi?" Elsu asked. "Our ancestors only spoke stories of those creatures. Never come across one in a hundred years."

"The markings on his arms were worrisome." Jacy's focus went to the window and the small shed in the backyard.

"They were magic." Elsu said.

Shay sipped at her tea and leaned forward. The only person she knew of with markings on his arms was that man at the casino. The one who'd dropped his French toast when he saw her. He didn't seem dangerous. She thought of Clyburn. But attractive men rarely let their demons shine through at the first meeting.

Maybe he was dangerous. Shay thought of the look on his face when they made eye contact. Slack jawed and… surprised. The French toast looked good after a few long days on horseback. She was disappointed for him that he'd dropped it. She touched the bandage near her ear. Whatever he saw in her, she doubted the tattooed guy would ever see it again. The big ugly scar across her forehead would put a stop to that. She sighed. It would take her out of the picture for many. She didn't want to rely on a man but she got the feeling she might have to lower her standards if push came to shove.

"When you are in doubt, be still and wait," Grandmother Crow was watching Shay from the opposite side of the kitchen. She gave Shay a look that made her think the old woman was reading her thoughts. "My stitching is better than most. Take care of the scar and it will barely be noticed."

Shay nodded.

There was a noise in the hall behind Shay. It had to be Clyburn walking. Shay scooted to the side and tried to hide. Grandmother Crow watched and frowned as Clyburn entered the kitchen.

Elsu waved for Clyburn to join them in the planning.

Shay's stomach lurched at the smell of chewing tobacco as he walked by.

Nicholas and the Crow men were talking about what to do with the tattooed guy.

"Kill him," Hosa said with disgust on his tongue. "The ancients said his kind killed plenty of ours in the wars."

Nicholas frowned and stroked his beard. "Enough have died in this mess. Kick him off your lands. Drop him at the edge of the reservation and tell him to never come back."

Hosa made a noise in his throat. "What if he brings

more of his kind? We are ill-equipped to handle the dead that walk and a war with giants."

"He's not that tall," Clyburn said as he sat in a club chair made of elk hide.

Hosa scowled. "His kin might be taller. Then what do we do?"

"What did he do to make you imprison him?" Nicholas asked.

"He set foot on our lands." Elsu crossed his arms and leaned back as though the charge was enough for prison.

"He didn't kill anyone?" Nicholas asked.

"Not yet." Hosa sounded convinced the guy was all sorts of dangerous.

"Let's focus on getting James a proper burial. Then we'll deal with the Allegewi." Iye seemed to be the only Crow brother with a level head.

Shay finished her tea and watched through the window. The shed didn't look like a prison but smoke rose from the center like a sweat lodge. Maybe they were trying to sweat the demons out of the guy.

CHAPTER 13

THE CROW MEN, NICHOLAS, AND CLYBURN LEFT for Lame Deer at three in the morning. They were confident the reservation was safe from the walking dead. The families that lived there were in close contact and well-equipped.

Shay enjoyed the time with Grandmother Crow. She slept soundly knowing Clyburn was gone and she wouldn't have to deal with him.

Shay was standing at the living room window, watching the sweat lodge smoke.

"Is there something in that shack that interests you?" Grandmother Crow asked as she clanked mugs onto the counter and set a pot of water on the stove to boil.

"What?" Shay turned. She wasn't sure how to respond. She was interested in the man with tattoos. She didn't think he was dangerous, but what did she know?

Grandmother Crow tipped her chin. "An Allegewi is something to be feared."

"Why do you call him that?" Shay asked as she crossed the room to help with breakfast.

"It's the name of the giants."

"How giant are we talking?" Shay asked.

Grandmother Crow tipped her shoulder, then raised her flattened hand. "Over six foot. Maybe eight."

The woman's heavily wrinkled face broke into a smile and she laughed. "Men worry about giants. The giants of a hundred years ago weren't much taller than the Crow men of this time."

"Why do they think he's dangerous?"

Grandmother Crow clucked her tongue. "They sense magic." She pointed the knife that she was cutting onion with. "I watched them bring him in. There is something. A blue shine to his skin." Her eyes narrowed on the sweat lodge. "Didn't you see it?"

Shay opened the tin of tea and set bags in each mug. "I'm not a Cheyenne. I'm just a basic white cowgirl. I don't see the world like you do, Grandmother Crow."

The old woman made a noise and went on with her cooking.

Shay was always out of place. She felt it every moment of her life. When she was at school, when she was at the store, when she was on vacation. She wasn't comfortable around most and the unrelenting voice in her head made her second guess most interactions. When she was with her parents or Nero, those were the only times she felt like maybe she belonged. Shay knew she needed to get out more. She needed to see the world and meet more people. Then maybe she'd feel like she belonged somewhere. Her forehead ached and Shay pressed fingertips to her temple.

No. That wasn't right. Her family would keep her safe. No matter what Shay wanted or thought, the truth was real. Her mother and father had gotten her this far. They'd taught her how to survive. They'd help her survive the walking dead until it was cleaned up and the world moved on like normal. Like it was before. Without her family and the ranch hands, Shay was nothing but a sitting duck in a screwed-up world.

"Don't rub it," Grandmother Crow said. "Try this." She sprinkled a black powder in Shay's mug.

Whatever Grandmother Crow sprinkled in Shay's tea helped with the headache. It also sent her right back to bed until dinner time. When Shay woke up, she could smell dinner cooking but didn't hear the voices of her father and the Crow men.

"They're not back yet," Grandmother Crow said as she stirred a pot.

"I'm going to check on Nero." Shay borrowed a heavy flannel jacket from near the door and went to the horse barn.

Nero neighed, happy to see Shay. "I know it's been a few days, boy." She patted Nero's neck and took a scoop of treats out of the nearby bin. Nero sniffed her bandages, and the horse tipped his head to the side as though he were inspecting her injuries.

"I'm fine." Shay spoke to Nero as she inspected the barn. She found her father's horse a few stalls down, as well as Clyburn's horse and James's. She gave treats to all of them and refilled their water. Doing the chores without flexing her facial muscles became a challenge.

When she left the barn, she headed toward the house

but the sweat lodge caught her eye. The guy was likely still in there. She focused on the smoke rising from the roof. Someone had to be refueling the fire. She walked to the nearby stack of firewood that was kept neatly under a covered section of the house. She picked up a log and headed toward the sweat lodge.

Shay pushed the door open slowly, using the end of the log. She wasn't sure what was going on in there. The Crow men had left and she hadn't noticed anyone visiting the backyard to check on the shed. The guy could be dead already or escaped.

The guy with tattoos all over his arms was there. He wasn't asleep and he wasn't tied up. He was just sitting by the roaring fire, reading from a small book, and chewing on dried meat.

"Hi," he said with a wave of a tattooed arm.

"Hi," Shay replied.

"I never thought I'd see you again." He closed the book and tucked it in his pocket.

"Same."

There was a pause as they studied each other. The air in the lodge became thick with questions and answers yet to be discussed. A need to know. An urge to explore. They stood that way for a long moment.

"Did the glass from the casino cut you?"

"What?" Shay asked.

He pointed to her head. "Your bandages."

Shay's hand flew to her head. "Oh. Yeah. The glass cut me and then later on, I fell off my horse."

"Are you okay?" he asked.

"I think so." Shay moved closer and dropped the log she

was carrying near the fire. "You dropped your toast back there."

The guy smiled.

Something melted inside of Shay.

"It was good French toast." A pink tongue darted out to lick his lower lip. "Too bad I won't be eating any of that again."

"Sad life with no French toast." Shay tried to contain her smile because she felt like a teenager. "They said you're a giant." She judged his height.

The guy made a face. "I'm taller than average. Not really a giant."

"Why don't they like you?"

"Plenty don't like me."

"What's your name."

"Jed. What's yours?"

"Shay."

"I like that. Did you come to rescue me, Shay?"

"I don't think so. But maybe I should. They discussed killing you."

"Killing me, huh?" He scooted forward in his seat then stood. His movements were slow, steady. He gave her time to leave before walking closer. "If I'm going to die. I guess I should do one last good deed."

He was a few feet from Shay but she didn't feel threatened. Instead she had an urge to reach out and touch him and make sure he was real. She searched for the blue glow to his skin that Grandmother Crow mentioned, but her eyes only saw pale, sweaty skin, dark ink, and smooth muscle.

Jed held his hands out, reaching to both sides of her head. "May I?"

Shay nodded and Jed removed the bandages from her head. The gauze stuck to the stitches, and she winced.

"Does it hurt?" Jed asked. His movements were slow and gentle.

"I've had worse. Broke my leg as a kid."

"Let me fix it." His voice was low and deep, nearly a hum.

Shay heard his fingertips tapping together and she watched his lips as he whispered strange words that sounded like a good promise. It made her ears tingle. Her skin felt warm, electrified. The tiny stitches fell down her face and Shay no longer felt the pulling of her skin. The wound tingled more and more, until it finally just, stopped.

"There," Jed said. "Just like before." His expression was something between wonder and deeply pleased. No one had ever looked at Shay that way before, besides her father.

Shay touched her forehead and was amazed when there were no stitches, no wound, no pain. He'd healed her.

"Why did you do that?" Shay asked. "How did you do that?"

"You're too pretty of a cowgirl to spend the rest of your life with a scar like that."

Shay looked at the tattoos on his arms. "Ok. But how?"

Jed held up his palms and wiggled his fingers.

"Magic?" Shay asked. "The Crow men said you had magic. I've never seen magic in real life. Only books and movies." Shay rubbed her forehead again, harder this time. She didn't feel any pain, no scarring or ache from the wound he'd healed.

Jed smiled as he stepped away. "Yeah. It's magic." The

reply was nonchalant, like magic actually existing wasn't a big deal.

"How?" Shay searched the room for anything that looked out of place, anything that could be an illusion and prompt her to wake up. This strangeness had to be a dream.

Jed bent and secured the clip on his bag. "How I did it is a long discussion. Probably one for another day."

The sound of truck engines and male voices ended their conversation. Jed began collecting items from where he'd sat near the fire and packed them into his bag. Before he could decide on which way to go, the front door of the shed blasted open. Along with it, came the brisk air of pending nightfall.

Chapter 14

It was Elsu. Shay sighed a breath of relief. Of all the Crow men, Elsu was the calmest. His dark eyes landed on Shay, then Jed.

"You untied him?" Elsu asked.

Shay raised her hands in innocence. "I didn't touch him." She took a few steps back, closer to the door and Elsu. "I swear."

Jed held his hands up in defeat. "She didn't. I did it myself."

"How?" Elsu asked.

Jed wiggled his fingertips. "I'm flexible. Handcuffs would have been more of a challenge."

Elsu's eyes narrowed on Jed. "You should have left while we were gone. It would have been better for you."

"Leave?" Jed smirked. "It's warm here." He motioned to the fire then the meat drying on the far wall. "There's plenty of food." He pointed to the door at the back of the room. "You even left me an old-ass bed. Probably got some fleas from sleeping on that thing. Why would I leave with hospitality like this?"

Elsu didn't respond. Shay's eyes widened and she tried not to smile at Jed's sarcasm.

"It's safe here," Jed said. "I can feel it in my bones."

"You might not think that much longer." Elsu opened the front door all the way and they could see the rest of the men unloading.

Clyburn crossed the ground and shoved his way into the shed. He grabbed Shay's arm and pulled her outside.

"Stop it," Shay hit his hand.

"Hey!" Jed shouted from inside. "Get your hands off her."

"What are you doing?" Clyburn asked Shay, bending so they were face to face. It was intimidating and made Shay's stomach lurch.

"Nothing." Shay pulled her arm back.

"What's going on?" Nicholas asked, dropping a load of gear.

"Nothing." Shay moved away from Clyburn and straightened her jacket. She wasn't sure how she was going to continue with his overprotectiveness turned jealousy. On this trip Clyburn had lost all apprehension of Nicholas protecting his daughter. He went full steam ahead with the closeness, the touching, the *saving*. Shay was tired of it. Clyburn didn't make her feel safe. It was quite the opposite. He felt like a threat; bottled up and shaken, ready to explode. Shay could sense it and she didn't want to be around when it happened.

"Let's get rid of the Allegewi now," Hosa said. "We can burn two bodies at once."

An unease spread through the Crow family. It wasn't like the Cheyenne to demand death so confidently. Grandmother Crow had made her way to the back porch and looked over her sons as they argued.

Elsu had made his way out of the shed. Jed stood in the doorway threshold, free as a bird, eyes bright as he took in the family argument of his impending death.

Iye and Jacy argued right along with the other brothers.

"We've already lost James."

"He'll kill more."

"His kind will come for us. They always have."

"It's been over a hundred years since the Allegewi warred with Cheyenne."

"Doesn't mean they aren't willing to start again."

Grandmother Crow didn't offer her opinion.

"We'll take him off your lands," Nicholas offered. "No one deserves to die in these times. Enough have died already."

"What–" Clyburn started, but Nicholas cut him off with a raised hand.

"He's already tainted Shay." Hosa said with a sneer.

"Hey," Nicholas growled. "Off limits."

Hosa pointed to Shay's healed head wound.

All eyes were on Shay. She stood steady as they inspected her forehead.

"Did it hurt?" Nicholas asked.

"I didn't feel a thing." Shay glanced at Jed.

"That's not natural. There is something wrong with this world. Something broken." Nicholas said.

"Our medicine has healed great wounds." Grandmother Crow said as she stepped down off the porch. "I gave her the black powder. How do you know it wasn't me who healed her?" Grandmother Crow stared hard at each of her sons. "My medicine has been called magic before."

Jed tipped his head down in respect to the old woman. He was sure she knew much about healing plants and poultices that the modern world had forgotten.

Just as quickly as it began, the conversation of Shay's healed wound was forgotten. No one wanted to argue with Grandmother Crow.

"I'd like to stay for James's burial," Nicholas said. "He was like a brother to me." He looked at Grandmother Crow.

"White man cannot come to the burial," Hosa said.

There was a muffled moan. Everyone focused on the open door of the truck bed, and the cloth covering James moved.

Chapter 15

———

"We waited too long," Clyburn said. "He's come alive again."

Shay had never seen it happen in real time; a man being dead then coming back to life. She'd only seen the ones who'd walked too close to the ranch and the horde that had busted into the casino. She'd seen James's corpse devoid of life back there. But now, now he was moving again.

Guttural groans were muffled from the cloth covering his body. James rocked and rolled off the truck bed onto the ground with a thud.

Clyburn was closest. He grabbed the sheet covering James and pulled it off his face. Jaws snapped. Clyburn jumped back and held a hand over his nose.

"Black powder won't fix that," Grandmother Crow said as she ran to safety on the porch.

Jacy took three long strides, dropped to his knee, and slammed a hunting knife through James's skull. The corpse stopped moving.

"Better bury him quickly," Iye said, collecting firewood

from the pile and loading it into the back of the truck.

Jacy and Elsu covered James's body and put him next to the firewood.

They took the body to the edge of the Crow family property. The men spoke and danced in ritual. Grandmother Crow chanted a prayer that Shay couldn't translate, even with her knowledge of some Cheyenne language.

Nicholas paid his last respects to his friend from a distance and the group decided they would head back to the ranch first thing in the morning.

Jed was left to the sweat lodge.

Shay slept soundly on a cot in Grandmother Crow's room.

They were used to waking up early and all were packed and ready to travel before the Montana sun rose.

They ate a quiet breakfast before heading to the barn to collect their horses.

Elsu brought Jed and Hosa was nowhere to be seen. It was better that way, Shay thought. Hosa would probably kill Jed with all of his anger bottled up.

Nero was happy to see Shay and pawed the ground with excitement at being saddled and released.

Nicholas and Clyburn collected their horses and secured their bags.

When they were ready to travel, Nicholas looked at Jed.

"I don't have a horse," Jed said with a shrug. "I can walk."

"You can ride with me," Shay offered. Nero was a big enough horse. He could carry them both. And Shay wanted to talk to him more.

"No," Clyburn said. "Shay can ride with me. He can

take Nero."

"I'm riding Nero." Shay scowled.

"You will ride with me," Clyburn seethed. His grip tightened on Shay's arm.

Shay stopped struggling and raised her chin.

"Come on." Clyburn tugged her, hard.

Shay couldn't take the ranch hand for one more second. The sweet smell of his chewing tobacco made her stomach churn. She had concluded that her family would keep her safe in all of this mess, but she couldn't stand one more second of Clyburn.

Shay swung her right arm as hard as she could and slapped Clyburn across the face.

The Crow men and Nicholas didn't stop their side conversations when Clyburn was man-handling Shay, but they did when they heard the clap of her open palm on his face.

"I am not your property," Shay said, bitterness on her tongue.

Something changed in Clyburn's eyes. It wasn't realization or remorse. It was anger.

Shay did something she never thought she'd have to do. She pulled the handgun from the holster at her hip, cocked it, and held the barrel under Clyburn's chin.

"Don't ever touch me again," Shay warned. She pressed the barrel harder. "Never again."

Clyburn raised his hands in defeat and backed up. "Good luck surviving this alone."

"I'm not alone. I have my daddy and momma. I definitely don't need you."

Clyburn's sleeve fell as he backed away and Shay saw a

hint of reddened skin.

"Shay-baby." Nicholas tapped Shay on the shoulder. "Put it away."

"Why, daddy?" Shay asked. "You offered me up like a new pair of shit kickers."

Clyburn backed away, dropped his hands, and went to ready his horse.

"I told you I wasn't interested in no ranch hand." Shay holstered her gun and turned to her father.

"I'm sorry. I just wanted to make sure you are taken care of. I won't be around forever." He pressed his lips together, weary.

Shay noticed the dark circles under her father's eyes. The wrinkles on his face seemed deeper, his clothes hung a little looser. "Are you sick or something?" Shay asked.

"No." Nicholas wrapped an arm around her. "Just getting older every day."

"I'm not some property to trade, daddy." Shay never thought she'd have to have a conversation like this. "Don't ever try to sell me off again."

Elsu came forward, passing reins to Nicholas. "Here, take James's horse. He'd want you to keep him."

"That's very kind of you." Nicholas ran his hand over the horse's dappled coat. "Have you ridden before?" he asked Jed.

"A long time ago," Jed said. He secured his foot in the stirrup and hauled himself up. It took Jed a minute to get the horse under control, but he managed better than most new riders. The last time he'd ridden, it was with Declan, the last Nephilim he'd come across. Since then the world had changed. Travel by horseback was outdated and as Jed traveled the northeast, he'd never found the need to travel by horseback since.

Jed stroked the horse's mane. The smell of warm leather and the horse brought back a lot of memories. Out of habit, Jed searched the sky for Angels or Demons.

"Let's go." Nicholas led the way.

They took a path through the foothills, avoiding Lame Deer entirely. When the path became harder to follow, near the thicker trees, Jed asked, "How do you know where the trail goes through these parts?"

Nicholas pointed to a tree with its trunk bent at a ninety-degree angle. "Trail markers. Just look for them."

They crossed Spotted Elk Drive and Sweet Medicine Road without seeing another soul. This wasn't uncommon on a normal Montana day. It was just the walking corpses had them all on edge. They started smelling the Waste Treatment station while crossing Ghostdancer Drive.

Jed coughed at the stench.

"We'll be upwind soon," Shay said as she slowed Nero.

"Can't tell if it's rotting corpses or shit," Jed said.

"Probably shit," Nicholas said.

Clyburn had been eerily quiet as he rode behind everyone.

They reached US-212 by lunch.

"If we keep going, we can be home by nightfall," Nicholas said.

"I'm sure momma is worried," Shay said.

Nicholas nodded. "Clyde too."

They galloped across the road and took the familiar route from a few days prior.

Jed glanced down US-212. He needed to get to California; he'd already been delayed by a few days with the Casino and Crow men. He watched Shay and thought of the man named Clyburn who was a few yards behind them. Something wasn't right and Jed didn't want to leave Shay in danger. Usually, Jed was quick to move on, but he did something out of the ordinary when he'd healed Shay's wound and now he felt compelled to make sure she made it home safely.

There was some strange energy in the air and Jed was sure it came from Clyburn. He couldn't leave Shay right now. Jed decided he'd make sure she made it home then he'd carry on. He'd have two good deeds for the week and could move on without regrets.

———

Shay didn't have what many would call a normal childhood. While she attended the local schools, she was frequently pulled out of class and missed days when a fresh load of cattle came in, or the gardens were ready for harvest and processing, or canning season was underway. She had a few friends when she was near ten, and they'd ride their bikes up and down the dusty roads searching for adventures. They drifted apart with time. After high school it became harder to keep in touch when the girls went to Texas and Florida for college and never returned to Colstrip, Montana. The calls and texts became less frequent until they stopped all together. Less than a year was all it took. Shay finally worked up the urge to apply to college and branch out.

One day she was packing her bags, ready to leave the

nest. The next, reports of the dead walking and spreading their death was all over the news.

"You can't go," momma argued.

"I have to go. I have to do something with my life," Shay said.

"You can do it here," her daddy said.

"I don't want to do it here. I want my own life. I want more than a life on a ranch in the middle of nowhere Montana," Shay said. "Everyone has left. I have no one here."

"You have us," Momma said.

"It's not the same." Shay didn't want to stay. She'd worked hard to get into the Biological Sciences undergraduate program. She wasn't going to throw it all away.

As Shay argued with her parents, she could hear the pounding of hammers as the ranch hands built up the fence and gate to the property. Momma had been stocking up on food for her whole life. Daddy had been stocking up on guns and bullets, traps, and knives. They were probably the most prepared ranch in the state.

Shay ran off. She didn't make it far. She stopped at a dive bar outside of Lame Deer, something her parents told her never to do. It didn't take long for the cowboy with dark hair and charisma to buy her drinks. It didn't take long for him to invite her back to his truck.

"I'm just traveling through," he'd said.

Shay didn't care. Her life was ruined by the dead walking. As far as she was concerned, this was her last hurrah. She didn't say no when the drunk cowboy tugged at her clothes and hoisted her up against the side of his truck. She didn't correct him when he called her by every name that started with an S besides Shay. She wasn't sure she ever told him her name. She never asked for his. Not when she unbuckled his belt. Not even when he was holding back her hair as she puked in the parking lot.

After, Shay went home with a new understanding of the world. Then three days later Clyburn showed up at the ranch looking for a work. Since another ranch hand vacated his post a few days prior, her parents were eager for help. And with his charming smile and muscular build, it didn't take her parents long to bring him onboard. They had an empty barracks and plenty of work for a healthy man.

Shay never told her parents she'd met the man that night at the bar. Neither did Clyburn. She ignored him and hoped he wouldn't remember. Shay hid in her room or the horse stalls. She avoided the farm hand at all costs. But that only lasted so long. The ranch was only so big and when their paths crossed, Clyburn recognized her and his relentless pursuit began.

Shay hated herself for running out that night. She wished she'd never met the ranch hand.

———

After a few hours of riding, they stopped to rest the horses at Castle Rock Lake. Jed asked Nicholas about the nearby strip mines and history. Nicholas seemed to like the conversation. It was the most Shay had heard her father talk in a long time. Jed had a real knack for chatting people up.

Clyburn moved closer to Shay, his movements so quiet she didn't hear him until he was right behind her.

"We should talk," Clyburn said.

"We have nothin' to talk about," Shay said.

"Look, I'm sorry I came on so strong." He sighed as he took off his hat. Dark hair fell over his eyes and he ran his hand through it. "I didn't mean to scare you."

"I've got nothin' to say to you." Shay took Nero's reins to feel secure in the moment. A horse was as good of a security blanket as anything. A baseball bat with nails might be better but she'd settle for a two-thousand pound stallion.

"We have something," Clyburn dropped to a knee.

Shay's stomach sank. No. No. No. No. "Don't you dare." She backed away. "We are nothing. There is nothing between us." She was embarrassed, panicked, couldn't believe this was happening.

"I'll tell your daddy about that night. I bet he'd see his Shay-baby in a new light." He rocked back on his heels and acted like he wasn't just about to pop the question after Shay had held a gun to his chin and threatened to blow out his brains through the top of his skull a few hours earlier.

"You shut your mouth," Shay warned, hand resting on the handgun at her hip.

Nero tugged Shay away and she happily went. She followed the horse who seemed to know better for her than that man.

She made it past the cluster of trees and sand where Nicholas and Jed's conversation had stopped as they watched her. Shay's legs were wobbly, her hands tingling with anger and fear.

"You okay?" Nicholas asked.

"That one needs his head examined." Shay thumbed toward Clyburn in the distance. "Keep him away from me."

Chapter 16

Then

"Jedidiah James Porter." The man in the corduroy coat and gold-rimmed glasses said his name like he was tasting wine.

"That's me," Jed replied. "In the flesh." Part of the name was fake, but he had forged papers.

"Hm."

Jed was hoping the man couldn't see the blue aura. Rarely anyone could, but some did. And when they could, it brought plenty of questions.

"Why do you want to work at the Peabody Library? We rarely see young men like you looking to mop floors at night."

"Well, any work is good work, sir." Jed nodded, hoping that was enough.

It wasn't.

Jed continued. "I like the books. I read. A lot. Um..." He was really losing traction here. Jed paused and cleared his throat. "I want to work. I don't mind mopping floors and cleaning. It's a starting point."

Papers shuffled. "Yes, we all need a starting point. Do you drink?"

"No."

"Get yourself into trouble?"

"No."

"Show up on time?"

"Always."

"Good. You're hired." The man stood and held out a hand to shake. "I'm John Vernon. I'll be your supervisor. Let's get you started."

"Thank you very much, sir."

Jed was hoping a new start was all he needed. He found trouble and sometimes it prevented him from showing up on time. Hell, the longest Jed held a job down was two years. It seemed like a lifetime ago. He'd done odd jobs on his travels to Maryland, hoping that warmer weather and salty air might help his predicament.

He knew it wouldn't, but it was a good lie to tell himself.

John walked Jed through the old library. There were signs for classes and meetings. The further into the building the quieter it got. They passed rooms with closed doors for private reading.

"Bathrooms are back here." John pointed to a metal sign hanging from the ceiling. "Each floor has them located in the same place. Made it easy on the plumbers when they built the place."

Jed nodded, his footsteps echoing in the expansive room turned large hallway.

"Locked section. You'll need a key to get in there at night."

Through the etched glass, Jed saw the shadow of a man walking with an enormous book in his hand. Maybe all the answers he needed in life were in there? Behind a glass wall and a metal lock. Jed's fingers twitched in his pocket. He had a certain luck with breaking into locks.

"Back here is where you'll find the offices and supplies." Keys jangled as John unlocked a door with a golden sign that said, *Employees Only*.

John led him down more halls; the walls turned to gray tile, the floors bare cement, the lights changed from decorative chandeliers to simple fixtures with a bare, single bulb. It was cold in this area of the library.

"There's the private collection room." John pointed to a steel door. "There's more storage down here. You wouldn't believe the things that show up at the library. Books from different countries, different eras, art, scrolls with claims that they're from the beginning of time." John chuckled. "Absurd."

The men finally stopped at a door with a wooden sign that read, *Janitor*.

John opened the door. "Declan, you in here?"

There was a rustling sound and footsteps. The room smelled like soap and brass polish. Jed had never experienced the two scents together, but he liked it. Strong enough to wipe out anything unpleasant but didn't burn the nose.

"Ahoy." A deep voice came from behind wooden shelves. "Excuse my–" The voice paused.

Jed knew why, instantly. The man named Declan had

the same blue aura as Jed. They stared for just a moment before Declan looked at John.

"This is Jedediah Porter, our new janitor." John clapped Jed hard on the back. "He's replacing poor old Henry. Them boots will be hard to fill." John made his way to the door. "Show Jed around. He'll be starting on night shift tomorrow." John held onto the door and where his fingertips pressed, Jed saw a strange little mark carved into the wood. "Welcome aboard, Jedediah." He tipped his head and left.

When John's footsteps were far enough down the hall that they could barely be heard, Declan crossed the room and closed the door, locked it, then turned to Jed.

"What are you doing here?"

"I came for a job."

Declan's eyes drifted over Jed, nostrils flaring above a red mustache that had been waxed to points. "I know what you are. We shouldn't be here together. It's dangerous. I've spent a very long time getting comfortable here and you're not going to ruin it for me."

"I don't know what you're talking about." Jed pointed to Declan's shoulders. "I didn't know there were any more like me alive."

Declan's shoulders dropped. His expression changed from anger to recognition.

"How old are you?" Declan asked.

"Twenty, sir."

"How long have you been running?"

"Since I can remember." Jed kept his face still, he didn't want to reveal anything even if this was the first time in his life that he felt safe. There was something about the library and this room that set Jed at ease.

"My apologies. I didn't realize you were nothin' but a babe." Declan opened his arms and hugged Jed like an old friend, like close family.

Jed couldn't have hugged the man back even if he tried, because his arms locked straight against his ribs as Declan squeezed. "Thank you," Jed said.

"Which Archangel fathered ya?" Declan pulled out a wooden chair and motioned for Jed to sit.

"I don't know." Jed sat, noticing strange carvings under the lip of the table and chair seat.

"Your mother?" Declan sat opposite.

"Died when I was a child."

Declan nodded. "That's usually what happens. They run with the baby until they get caught." Declan pointed one finger at Jed. "But, she must've been running with you for a long time if you got old enough to take care of yourself."

"Yes, sir."

Memories came flooding back. Memories that Jed had buried deep down. Dark nights and hurried movements, his mother's hushed voice saying, "We have to go, baby." Horse hoofs running on soft dirt, the moon revealing shadowed beasts that no child should see. The smell of her as Jed buried his face in her clothing, arms tight around her middle.

His mother had learned to fight, taught herself how to wield a sword, then various knives that she could keep hidden in her skirts. She was good at finding food and safe places to sleep. She taught him how to run, how to recognize the change in the air when an Angel or Demon had broken through realms, the whisper of their wing beats, and the deception of an angelic face.

"Use your luck," she would say to get into hotel rooms or empty houses. Sometimes she would wash his face and trim his hair and set him on the street with a tin can. Everyone gave him money. "What a handsome boy," they'd say, dropping coins into his tin. But his looks and his luck only got them so far. He couldn't protect her. He couldn't save her that night.

"Do you know any tricks yet?" Declan asked.

"I can pick a lock."

"We can do better than that." Declan raised his hands, chanted strange words, and tapped his fingertips together. The saltshaker on the table rose in the air and floated across the room. Declan grinned, wide and satisfied.

"Can you show me how to do that?" Jed asked. He didn't want to sound desperate, but he was. Jed was desperate to survive as more than just a man on the run.

"Boy, I can show you so much more."

———

Declan taught Jed more than how to mop floors at the Peabody Library. Jed's nights were filled with learning Nephilim magic. He had more than just dumb luck and a pretty face. Declan made sure he learned it all.

"What are these markings?" Jed asked, his fingers rubbing the wooden doorframe where he'd just polished.

"You rubbed off the spell." Declan took a sliver of chalk out of his pocket and wrote strange markings on the threshold. The markings faded into the woodwork. "This is how we stay alive, boy."

Lessons on cleaning turned into lessons about spells and runes. "I keep track of them in this book." Declan showed Jed a small, leather-bound book he kept in his pocket.

Deep in the bowels of the library, there were hidden rooms that had been long forgotten. Declan helped Jed set up his own. He showed Jed how to carve runes of protection into the woodwork, what spells to write on the walls with chalk, that a line of coarse salt could protect or trap. Jed had never slept so soundly in all of his life.

Jed read every book, studied every ancient bible and text in the building.

"There, that one." Declan pointed to a page that Jed was reading. "That one is my father."

Remiel.

"He enjoyed the red-haired women of the Isle." Declan sat with a steaming cup of coffee he'd taken from the lobby. "That's how I survived. They don't like the boats." He took a sip from the mug. "Or at least they didn't."

"You don't sound Irish," Jed said.

"When you've been around for longer than you should, one learns to hide their native tongue."

———

"I've got some bad news for you, boys." John Vernon was standing in front of Jed and Declan. His face hallowed, skin pale, clothes threadbare. "Peabody Library is closing. We're all out. They're closing the doors until the Depression passes. Don't know how long it will be. You're both welcome to come back. Could be a few years, could be ten." John exhaled a haggard breath.

Dread filled Jed. He'd been safe for the first time in his life and now it was all being taken away. No more nights reading. No more lessons in magic casting. No more.

"We've got about a week to clean up and convert the rooms to storage. Then I'll need you both out of here."

"Sure thing." Declan's voice had too much hope in it.

Jed wanted to scream.

CHAPTER 17

THEN

PEOPLE DO STRANGE THINGS WHEN THEY THINK the world is ending. Some drink themselves into oblivion. Some loot and riot and kill and fuck. When man is pushed to the edge, they can turn into beastly things. Some might say God lived in Heaven because he feared the beasts he'd created. Or maybe he feared the monsters with wings and scales that liked to meddle on his Earthen plane and that was why he didn't intervene the night Clyburn summoned a lesser Demon at the crossroads in the middle if a starry sky Montana night. What was one meddlesome Demon? Plenty had escaped to wreak havoc.

Clyburn feared death more than anything and he made a deal with a demon to come upon a homestead that was safe, secure, and prepped for the apocalypse that was starting. He also asked for a woman to live out the rest of his life with. What is a man without a woman? Adam and Eve were first, Clyburn was going to make sure he and Shay were the last.

"I want a deal," Clyburn said to the winged creature in front of him.

"A deal will cost you." The lesser demon's voice was smooth as whiskey. He scraped an X into the center of the crossroads with a taloned foot.

"Whatever you want." Clyburn would not die like the others. He was going to live, no matter what. He wasn't going to be bit, suffer, die, and be born again as a rotting corpse. No, he had more self-respect than that.

"Out of the eater will come something to eat. And out of the strong will come something sweet." The Demon smiled and held out a dusky hand with long necrotic finger-nails and a golden ring on its middle finger.

"You want me to give you food?" Clyburn asked.

"You said anything. Something sweet. Something to eat. Shake on it."

The Demon's necrotic index finger scraped the soft inner skin of Clyburn's wrist as they shook on it. Etched in darkness, the deal was done.

CHAPTER 18

There was only a sliver of daylight remaining in the sky when the travelers reached the ranch outside of Colstrip.

The old ranch hand, Clyde, was using a dagger taped to a stick to clear the dead from pushing on the fence.

"Where'd they all come from?" Shay asked her father.

"Must've wandered this way. Won't be the first time. He cleared his throat headed for a crop of trees to tie up the horses. "We better clear them out before nightfall."

Clyburn, Jed, and Shay followed Nicholas. They moved quickly and quietly, chopping off the heads of the handful of zombies that had amassed. They dragged the bodies a good few hundred yards away from the ranch to a ditch Nicholas had dug months prior. They tossed the bodies in and lit them on fire.

Shay covered her nose with her shirt. The smell of burning human flesh was awful. She'd helped clear the fence before but there had never been so many at once.

Black smoke rose and she hoped it wouldn't bring more of the dead.

"Let's go see momma," Nicholas said, bumping shoulders with Shay.

"I've missed her," Shay said. "She's probably worried."

They collected their horses and headed for the gate.

Clyde and Momma were waiting for them. Clyde swung open the gate then quickly closed it when they were through.

"I was so worried," Momma said as she kissed Shay's cheek. She looked Shay over for injuries, motioning to her dusty clothes before turning her attention to Nicholas. "Did you find James?"

"We found his body," Nicholas said. "Crow family put him to rest. Grandmother Crow says hello. She sent a few things for you."

Nicholas handed over a small bag filled with teas and herbal medicines.

"And who might you be?" Momma asked Jed as she looked him over, eyes stopping at the ink on his arms.

Jed introduced himself.

"He's just staying the night," Nicholas said. "Wanted to make sure we made it back safe and sound. He'll be moving on now that he's out of Cheyenne territory."

"Glad you're home," Momma said to Clyburn as he passed her, taking his horse to the barn.

Clyburn nodded and flashed a charming smile.

Momma focused on Jed again. "Dinner's ready, I'll go put out an extra plate. Why don't you all put the horses away and wash up?"

Momma headed for the house and Nicholas broke off

in conversation with Clyde, updating him on what they'd seen in Lame Deer.

"Come on," Shay said to Jed. "I'll show you where the horses sleep."

She held Nero's reins loose as they walked to the barn. Shay thought it had been a long time since she hadn't run to the barn to hide from Clyburn.

"So this is where you live?" Jed asked.

"Yup." Shay's face pinched. "Boring, right?"

"Nah, it's nice." Jed pointed to the high fence surrounding the property. "Have you always had that, or did you all build it just for the dead?"

"It's always been there. Daddy was always planning for something like this to happen. Between the TV shows and movies, he got it in his head that something dire was coming. He and Momma built the ranch to withstand anything."

"Anything?" Jed's brows rose. "Like a nuclear bomb?"

Shay shrugged. "We have a small underground space." She pointed to a tiny shed in the distance. "You just have to get there in time."

"Damn." Jed rubbed his neck. "What about food?"

"Root cellars. Everything is canned. And we have the gardens and the animals." A rusty-colored hen waddled across their path. "Plenty of chickens and eggs."

"Seems Nicholas has it all figured out."

"Some things." Nero nudged Shay as they walked. "You want carrots?" she asked the horse.

Nero neighed and huffed. Clyburn was walking back to the house, giving them a wide berth as he passed.

Shay figured the horses were exhausted after their travels. She sure was. A few days on the road is tiring enough, let alone adding in danger and distress–Shay touched her forehead–and magic.

"Why did you come back to the ranch with us?" Shay asked.

"Well, your Crow friends were going to skin me alive. I figured they needed some time to cool off. And I wanted to make sure you got home safe." Jed turned and checked for Clyburn. "Seems you have some trouble with that ranch hand."

Shay huffed out a laugh. "You could say that again."

They entered the horse barn and Shay showed Jed where to hang the reins and saddles. They changed the water and gave the horses fresh oats and carrots.

Shay noticed Jed didn't let his bag out of sight while they worked. He kept it on his back or slung over one shoulder.

They washed up at the well pump that was near the house.

Shay could hear Nicholas's booming laughter as he told Momma about their travels.

Clyburn was wandering the wraparound porch.

Shay avoided him by taking the long way to the dinner table, through the back door and hallway. She led Jed along.

"Smells good," Jed said as the floorboards creaked under their feet.

"Momma's a superb cook. It smells like lasagna."

Dinner was lasagna, served with a side of uncomfortable shoulder rubbing when Clyburn took the seat next to Jed. Shay was relieved the ranch hand didn't sit next to her. She sat next to Momma and couldn't believe how much she'd missed the warmth of her mother's personality. Shay glanced at her parents as they talked through dinner and held conversation with everyone at the table. James was a topic of discussion for much of the meal. Then Clyde told them about the horde that had passed by the ranch.

"We tried to stay quiet, but those damn roosters," Momma said as she took a sip of wine. "We might have to make chicken soup out of them all." She shook her head. "They came for the roosters. What if the cow was mooing?"

"Rooster soup," Nicholas joked. He watched out the window. Shay knew that look; he was strategizing. "We'll have to do something about the roosters, I guess."

"There's a weak spot in the fence," Clyde said. He pointed with is fork. "Northwest corner. I reinforced it as well as I could, but it needs cement poured."

"We'll fix it in the morning," Nicholas said.

When they were done eating, everyone helped clean up. The table was cleared, and dishes done in thirty minutes.

Shay avoided Clyburn, even when her mother asked, "Why does he keep looking at you like that?"

"I threatened to kill him," Shay whispered back as she dried a plate then set it in the cupboard.

Momma laughed but stopped short when she saw the serious look on Shay's face. "Details. Later." Momma glanced to Jed who was sweeping under the dining table. "What about that guy?"

"I'm not sure yet." Shay hid her smile.

"He's very nice to look at."

"Momma, you're married."

"That doesn't mean I can't look." She watched Jed bend over to sweep debris into a dustpan.

CHAPTER 19

Then

THE FIRST FEW YEARS OUTSIDE OF PEABODY WERE the hardest. There were no jobs in the city. Jed and Declan went to the Maryland coast and traveled north. They stopped in Chesapeake City and found work fishing on the canal.

Darkness was everywhere during the Depression. Hell was an open hand waiting for anyone who would take it.

They used charcoal to etch the runes of protection into the seams of their clothing and the insides of their shoes. And so the progression of Declan and Jed's survival methods evolved.

"Hey," Declan threw a live crab at Jed. "Dare you to sell that to the woman at the bank."

Selling crabs was an ongoing gig between the two. Sometimes the coin was good, sometimes they gave them away for free to the hungry children.

Jed flicked the rim of his fedora and lit a cigarette. The tip burned brightly in the darkness.

"The woman at the bank?" Jed asked, picking up the crab. "With the red dress?"

"Wouldn't recommend anyone else for your cheekbones." Declan chucked and clapped the other fisherman.

"Ye can sell her this little fella." The other fisherman held up a giant Rockfish and wiggled it.

"I'll take my chances with the crab." Jed bent and picked it up. Pinschers snapped at his fingers. He picked up the crab by a leg and dangled it. "The bank lady could eat you in one bite."

"Could say the same for you boy," Declan slapped Jed on the back as the boat hit the dock.

The men collected the morning's fishing and headed for the pier. It was cold, but the walk in would warm their bones from the ocean chill.

They sold their fish and paid their dues to the boat owner. The men went home to a tiny, rented house on the bad side of town where the weeds were always taller than the flowers and the shrubbery looked anemic and ready to die. Jed grabbed the crab out of the sink and headed for the door.

"You're gonna do it?" Declan asked.

"Never backed down from a challenge."

Declan laughed and shouted vulgar encouragements as Jed left.

The woman in the red dress left the bank at the same time every day. Jed rarely ventured out alone, but he felt safe in their current routine. Not as safe as Peabody, but it would do. The nightmares of the day his mother died were fewer and further between. And while Jed knew better than to put down roots, the thought of a good woman on his arm was something he'd like to experience before he died.

Townspeople stared as he passed them. The women covered their mouths to whisper to each other. Jed knew it was his height and looks. He stopped at the bank and looked through the window. The woman in the red dress was at the counter. He went inside.

"Can I help you?" she asked.

Jed read her nametag. Eileen.

"Good afternoon, Eileen." He smiled. "I'd like to make a withdrawal."

"Sure. Do you have your account number?"

"No."

"Do you have an account here?"

"No but I have this crab." He set the creature on the counter.

"It looks sick."

"It knows death is coming." Jed stroked the crab with calloused fingers. "But that doesn't stop it from wanting a night with a beautiful lady."

The conversation morphed from simple greetings to a date. Eileen left for work in thirty minutes.

Jed gave the crab to a hungry stranger on the street then he went and reserved a table at the Italian restaurant down the street.

After dinner, Jed was charming enough to get a kiss and a promise of another date. He walked Eileen to her house and waited for her to lock the door.

Jed began walking home. He paused when he felt an abnormal chill in the air. The energy changed. He reached in his pocket for the knife he always carried.

"You shouldn't be here." A dark voice whispered.

"Neither should you." Jed flicked the knife, whispered a spell that would make him invisible.

The creature explored the street, looking for Jed before it focused on the light coming from the house. Spikes stuck out of its back, hunched like a hedgehog with legs thick as tree trunks. It was a creature he'd never seen before. With the smell of creosote, it could only have come from one place. Hell.

"Mmmm." The dark creature began walking across the road.

Jed thought about running and hiding like he'd done when he was a kid. He hadn't faced a creature like this in a very long time. He was out of practice with fighting.

The creature settled one foot onto Eileen's stairs leading to the porch. "I smell you here." It said, "Inside." The creature scrambled up the steps to Eileen's door.

Jed ran toward the house. The creature crashed through the front door. Searching. Sniffing. Roaring. "Come out!"

Eileen screamed. Glass broke.

Jed leapt up the front steps two at a time and ran into the house, following the trail left by creature. He didn't have much of a plan besides to try and kill it or lead it away from Eileen. He jumped over a broken vase, a busted table. Debris led him to the kitchen in the back of the house.

He was too late.

Eileen was crumpled on the floor. Her red dress was ripped to shreds; giant claw marks had torn apart her middle.

CHAPTER 20

JED FOLLOWED NICHOLAS TO THE PRIVATE ROOMS for ranch hands.

"You want to reconsider staying?" Nicholas asked. "We could use the help. Strong guy like you would be perfect."

"Nah, I'm behind schedule, got to get to California to meet a friend."

"In this mess?" Nicholas made a face. "Is your friend still alive?"

If Jed was correct and the darkness that the horde was following was Sparrow he'd be well and alive, more so than anyone.

"It's all I can hope," Jed said.

Nicholas opened a rough-hewn door and walked inside the room. "There's a private bath and clean sheets."

"Better than I've had most nights." Jed checked the window for locks.

"Welp, if you change your mind or want to swing by again in your travels, you're more than welcome. After healing Shay, we more than owe ya."

Jed nodded and moved to close the door as Nicholas walked out.

"I'll expect you for breakfast," Nicholas said.

"See you then."

Jed closed the door to the room and took a breath. His stomach had never felt so full and after the long ride to the ranch, he more was exhausted than ever.

Jed settled on the bed and kicked his boots off. He told himself he was only going to rest his eyes for a few minutes, then he'd get up and place some wards for safety. His last thought before falling asleep was that he should have warded Shay's room as well.

CHAPTER 21

Clyburn had the room next door to Jed and with the thin, clapboard walls, he heard everything Nicholas was saying. Clyburn was getting anxious. He wanted more time to set things right, more time to get Shay on his side.

But time was running out. If Jed was leaving in the morning, he'd be back another time and it would be a surprise. Clyburn couldn't wait for surprises. He had to take matters into his own hands.

Clyburn left his room and walked down the hall of the guest area to the shared living room.

"Hey, man." Clyde tipped his beer and focused on the static television, searching for a channel that was broadcasting.

"Just stepping out for some fresh air," Clyburn said as he opened the door and closed it.

There was a chill on the Montana night. The moon was full and stars bright. Clyburn didn't need light for what he was about to do. He walked to the hen house, opened the door as silent as a fox and took out the fattest hen. He considered something bigger like the cow or a horse, but the hen would be easiest.

Clyburn went to the dirt path near the gate to the ranch. It was furthest from the house and hidden by three tall Ponderosa Pine trees. He scuffed an X into the dirt, took a knife from his pocket and sliced his hand, letting drops of blood fall into the middle of the X.

Then he waited.

Summoning a crossroads Demon wasn't common knowledge. It was a darkness no ranch hand knew how to call upon. He learned this dark magic from his grandfather. Clyburn's family was never rich or prosperous, but they survived. All it took was a little blood and a deal. It could pay bills, find the right job, pay off a lien, get a girl, kill a pesky neighbor. Clyburn's grandfather had used the crossroads Demon for all of the above in his lifetime. Unfortunately for Clyburn, not all deals were satisfied with death. Some were passed on to living relatives.

Clyburn waited and waited and waited for the Demon to rise from the X. He checked his watch. Thirty minutes. He exhaled a breath of frustration, but his eye caught movement in the upper window of the ranch house. Shay was walking through her bedroom getting ready for bed. Clyburn watched her. "Mine," rumbled out of his mouth.

"What's yours? Is it sweet?" the familiar voice of the crossroads Demon asked.

"Here." Clyburn held out the hen. "If you need something to eat, this is sweet enough."

The Demon showed sharp teeth as he took one step and inspected the surrounding ranch. The Demon dropped to all fours, like a panther scheming. He made a sound deep in his chest, something that sounded like a chant.

"Hey," Clyburn snapped, trying to refocus the Demon.

A long, bifurcate tongue tasted the Montana air. The X on the dirt opened up, earth crumbled and fell into the hole that appeared. Three hands reached up, grasped for purchase, and pulled themselves up.

"What are you doing?" Clyburn asked. Panic began flooding his veins. He knew better than to trust these things.

The crossroads Demon sniffed the air. "Out of the eater will come something to eat. And out of the strong will come something sweet."

"This is not our agreement." Clyburn reached for his gun.

The crossroads Demon hissed, kicked out a leg, its foot connecting with Clyburn's chest, sending him flying into a tree trunk. His head hit with a sickening thud. His body rolled into the hole where the X had opened up.

The Demons crouched close to the ground, scurrying like cockroaches, headed for the main house.

Chapter 22

Jed woke in the darkness with an uneasy feeling. He cursed himself for sleeping for so long. He'd only planned to rest his eyes like the old folks would say. Now the moon was high and shining through his open window.

Open?

Jed didn't leave the window open. He'd checked the locks and had planned to set some wards but never did.

The floorboards creaked.

Jed knew that uneasy feeling he'd woken with. He wasn't alone in the dark room. He glanced to his bag at the foot of the bed. He needed the big knife with the runes etched into it. Just as he had the thought, his bag started slowly moving, being pulled off the foot of the bed.

It was now or never.

Jed clapped his hands and twisted his fingers into shapes like stacked pyramids. He spat words that sounded like the hiss of fire igniting. Light erupted from the foot of the bed and as it did, Jed launched himself forward to grab his bag and pull the knife out. The creature on the floor scurried to the wall and hissed back.

"You don't belong here," Jed said.

The creature jabbered in Hellspeak. It sounded pissed and hungry.

Jed secured his bag over his shoulder, gripped the knife and moved toward the lesser Demon as it crouched, trying to escape the ball of light.

"What are you doing here?" Jed asked the Demon, settling the tip of the knife at the base of the Demon's throat.

"Something sweet to eat," it garbled.

"You don't belong on this plane." Jed slid the knife down the creature's neck, but stopped when he heard a struggle in the living room. "How many of you are there?"

"More than me."

"How many?" Jed pressed the tip of the knife in. It required more pressure to pierce the Demon's thick hide.

"We are four of the crossroads."

The ball of light was starting to fade. The Demon watched it, muscles twitching, ready to fight when it went dark again.

Jed slammed his knife through the Demon's heart. "Not today, shithead."

The Demon's body slouched against the wall and inky blood pooled between its legs on the floor.

Jed looked at the open window, then the door. Old habits were hard to break. He climbed out the window. Whatever happened in the living room, he was sure the other Demon had won from the sounds. The chewing of human bone was a distinct sound, and Jed was sure whoever was out there wasn't chewing on the Demon's bones.

Jed glanced at the gate to the ranch. He could be gone quickly and save his own hide. He'd done it enough times throughout his lifetime. He glanced at the main house and the window on the second floor.

Shay.

Damn it.

Jed knew better than to get attached. But he knew Shay would die if he left now. At least he could try. He remembered the feel of her energy under his palms as he healed her forehead, the glimmer in her eyes as she joked about saving him. No, he couldn't leave Shay to die. Being eaten by a Demon was never a good way to go.

Jed inched along the guest house exterior. He watched the shadows for movement.

One Demon slunk out of the front door of the guest house. Another left the horse barn. A third moved from the kitchen window inside the house.

Jed moved. He ran to the house. The other two Demons made it to the front door before him. They blasted through and began wrecking the interior of the house, searching for blood.

Jed began climbing the railing. He jumped to grab the roof overhang of the front porch and pulled himself up. Arms aching, he was running on pure adrenaline. He climbed onto the roof and went to Shay's window. He tried to open it, but the frame didn't move. He tapped on the glass.

"Shay, wake up," he said just above a whisper.

Jed didn't want to make too much noise and draw

attention, but he needed Shay to wake up or next he'd be breaking the window.

He tapped the glass harder. There was movement inside. On the bed, then the floor.

His stomach sank. He was too late.

But then footsteps moved closer. The window unlocked and opened.

"Jed?"

"Thank God you're okay." He moved back. "Get out here."

"Why?"

A large crash and the sound of Momma screaming broke through the night.

Shay ran back into the room. She rounded her bed and pulled a shotgun out from under the bed.

Without a chance of getting her out of the window, Jed climbed in.

"Shay," he warned. "There are creatures here."

"Oh no, the dead?" her face paled. "Are Momma and Daddy dead?"

"I don't know. But you're about to see something you've never seen before."

Jed was interrupted by the door blasting open. One demon charged into the room like a lion leaping to attack prey.

Shay shot it. Shotgun pellets left a blast hole in the creature's chest. She turned to Jed. "What the fuck was that?"

"A Demon." He moved closer to the corpse on the floor, used his knife to stab it through what was left of the heart, just to be sure. "Nice shot, by the way."

"Daddy didn't raise no sissy." Shay loaded the shotgun

chamber, opened her nightstand drawer, pulled out a box of shells and tucked them into her pocket.

They heard the sounds of Nicholas fighting and shouting from the bedroom downstairs.

Shay ran out of the room without another word. Jed followed.

Momma was lying in a pool of blood. One of the Demons crouched near her shoulder, feeding from her neck like a vampire.

"Get out!" Nicholas shouted as he grappled with the other Demon. Blood was dripping down the side of his head. "Run."

Both Demons turned to Jed and Shay. The one near Momma rose. "Out of the strong will come something sweet." The Demon focused on Shay, body twitching, ready to pounce.

Jed tried his previous spell; it subdued the first one. He clapped his hands and twisted his fingers. He spat the words that sounded like the hiss of fire igniting. Light erupted in the center of the room. The Demons shrieked and scurried to the far wall. Jed leapt over to the bed to confront the Demons.

"Who summoned you here?" Jed had a knife in each hand, tips touching the leathery necks of the beasts.

"One who desires what he does not have." The Demon's eyes flicked to Shay.

"A name." Jed pressed harder with each knife.

"Clyburn," the Demon hissed.

Jed recognized nothing special about Clyburn, just that the guy had a serious hard-on for Shay and no boundaries.

"What is Clyburn?" Jed pressed the tips of each knife until dark blood dripped from the necks of the Demons.

"A foolish man with a plan."

"Just a man?" Jed asked.

"Nothing more than Earthen plane scum," the Demon on Jed's left said as it began moving, trying to escape. The creature had grabbed a lamp cord and swung it, the lamp colliding with Jed's back.

"Move right," Shay shouted.

Jed stooped and twisted, felt the force of buckshot scrape the air.

The Demon to his left slid down the wall, head tipped to the side and half of its face and neck dripping.

Jed's ears were ringing. He shook his head, hoping it would pass. His hand was steady on the knife holding the last Demon.

"A deal is a deal." The Demon focused on Shay. "The ranch and the girl."

"Focus, creature." Jed slapped the Demon on the side of the head. "You can't have her."

"Out of the eater will come something to eat. And out of the strong will come something sweet. A deal is a deal." The Demon knew he was outnumbered. There was nothing but death for him in this room, but he was driven by desire for something he could never have on the plane of Hell. A fresh human to eat. Nothing was sweeter or more filling. The crossroads Demon was going to get what he was promised. Taloned feet dug into the carpet as he readied himself.

The ball of light in the middle of the room faded.

The creature launched himself, twisting away from the tip of Jed's knife.

Jed twisted, grabbed the Demon by its ankle, slammed it to the ground.

Nicholas grabbed the Demon's shoulders and helped hold it down.

Jed stabbed it in the heart. As the Demon was dying, it howled like a wolf in the night and a wisp of a soul left its body, flying out the broken window and disappearing into the moonlight.

Jed looked the Demon over, making sure it was dead. He touched its hand with the golden ring and chain connected to a golden bracelet. He rarely came across Demons wearing anything like this. Jed cut the Demon's arm at the wrist, just above the golden bracelet.

"What are you doing?" Nicholas asked.

"Saving this for later." Jed stood and went to the kitchen. He searched the cabinets and drawers for a large Ziploc bag and put the Demon hand inside.

When Jed returned to the bedroom, Nicholas and Shay stooped over Momma's body. Jed hadn't seen a man like Nicholas cry in a long time and he felt uncomfortable watching.

Jed waited in the hall as they said their goodbyes. Nicholas and Shay closed the bedroom door as they walked toward him.

"We should check the rest of the ranch and make sure we got them all," Jed suggested.

"There's more?" Shay asked.

"I killed four." Jed headed to the back door on the far end of the kitchen.

A black shadow galloped by.

"That's Nero." Shay ran forward and out the door.

"Wait," Nicholas ran after her.

Jed couldn't imagine losing everything in one night. That was why he didn't connect with people like this. It never ended well.

CHAPTER 23

Nero followed Shay as the survivors searched the ranch.

"So, you have magic," Nicholas said to Jed.

"I do." Jed was distant, his mind a million miles away. His first instinct was to run and save himself, but he couldn't this time. He watched Shay walk, one hand on Nero's flank. She seemed unfazed by what had occurred, while her father was nearly in shock. She fought by Jed's side and showed no fear of the Demons as they pursued her. Most of all, Jed's magic didn't scare her. Plenty of women wouldn't be able to compartmentalize what he was and what he could do. Shay hadn't seen most of it, but what little she'd experienced didn't scare her away. For the first time in his life, Jed wondered what life with a partner might be like.

"Didn't think that was real." Nicholas looked pale and the blood had dried on his face creating a crust. He didn't move to clean it off. "Those Crow boys weren't wrong."

"What in the actual fuck just happened?" Shay asked.

"Angels and Demons are real. The Demons are a bit uglier, sometimes." Jed said.

"Angels?" Shay turned to face him.

"Don't get all dreamy-eyed," Jed warned. "They aren't as wonderful as the movies make them out to be. They're just as deadly."

"Wonderful." Shay was looking at the front door to the ranch house. "First zombies, now Angels and Demons."

"We need to burn the bodies." Nicholas's eyes were focusing on the different parts of the ranch, calculating how to get everything done.

"Even the animal bodies?" Shay asked.

"Yes." Nicholas rubbed his face. "Better to be safe."

They all dreaded what the next few hours would bring.

———

THEY FOUND the bloodbath in the guest house: Clyde and the Demon from Jed's room. Jed, Shay, and Nicholas dragged the bodies to the dirt path near the gate to the ranch. Nicholas had moved his truck to bring the bodies to the ditch where they burned the other dead.

They piled on the dead chickens, goats, and the Demons from inside the main house. They had to tie up the corpse of the cow and drag it.

"Where's Clyburn's body?" Shay asked.

"I haven't seen him," Nicholas said. "We'll keep looking."

"Something could have taken him," Jed suggested, tossing a dead chicken into the back of the truck.

There were two dead walking across the prairie outside

the fence of the ranch. The noise of the truck engine turning over gave them focus and they began meandering toward the ranch.

Nicholas and Shay rode in the truck cab. Jed walked and took care of the dead things on his way to burn the bodies. He dragged the corpses to be burned with the rest.

"You think more will come?" Shay asked.

"Yup." Nicholas replied with a grunt as he tossed the goat into the burn pit.

"Goodbye old friend," Nicholas said as Clyde's body was tossed last. He lit a match and threw it into the pile of bodies. "Now for the worst part."

Shay knew what the worst part was. Getting Momma. She hadn't cried over the loss of her mother. There wasn't time to process it all. The grief was coming off her father in waves as he drove them back to the ranch. Black smoke rose in the distance as the bodies burned.

Shay and Jed waited by the truck as Nicholas went inside to take care of the woman he'd spent most of his life with.

"What can I do to help?" Jed asked.

Shay was staring off in the distance. "I don't think there's anything else you can do. You fought those things." She rubbed her face, stopped, and looked at her filthy hands. There was dirt smeared down her cheeks.

"Should it be taking him this long?" Jed asked, watching the front door.

Glass broke.

Shay ran inside. Jed followed.

"Daddy?" Shay shouted as she ran toward her parent's bedroom.

There were thuds against the walls.

Shay shoved the door open. "No."

Momma had turned.

Nicholas was struggling with what to do. Shay could see that he didn't want to put a final end to Momma. Nicholas had tried to put a pillowcase over her head, but it was only halfway down her face.

"Let me," Jed said, pushing Shay aside and striding across the room, hunting knife in hand. He jabbed it through the side of Momma's skull and her resurrected body dropped to the carpet.

"Christ," Nicholas said as he bent, head in his hands.

"We got this, Daddy," Shay said. "Why don't you go get some fresh air?"

Nicholas left the room. Shay heard him open the liquor cabinet and drop a glass on the floor. He swore. Kicked something.

Shay stooped and pulled the pillowcase down over Momma's face. Jed tore the top blanket off the bed and laid it on the floor. They rolled Momma's body onto the blanket, then rolled her up in it.

Shay took the cords holding the curtains back and used them to tie up Momma.

"Why don't you get her feet?" Jed suggested as he tested the weight of her shoulders.

Shay hiccuped and it sounded like a half-stifled cry.

"You know what? Let me try something else." Jed took the small book out of his pocket and flipped through the pages. He read one page for a minute before putting it away. He sang words that sounded like the rocking of ocean waves, his fingers tapped in constant movement. Momma's body rose from the floor. Jed moved her with his magic, his hands guiding her out of the room, down the hall, and out the front door. He settled her in the back of the truck, his arms dropping in fatigue.

"Thank you," Shay said.

Jed nodded nonchalantly, before sitting on the porch steps.

Chapter 24

"I NEED SOMETHING TO DRINK," SHAY SAID, touching Jed's shoulder as she walked up the steps to the porch. "You want some lemonade or something?"

"Sure." Jed nodded.

The screen door creaked then slammed closed as Shay walked into the house.

Shay found a pitcher and filled it with cold water from the tap. She found lemonade mix in the cabinet and added it to the water, mixing with a wooden spoon. There was one lemon on the counter. She cut it into wedges and added it to the pitcher. Reaching for the glasses, she heard footsteps behind her.

"I would have brought it out to ya," Shay said, taking down a glass and filling it. "Do you want ice?"

A strange groan came from behind her. The floorboards creaked.

Shay turned and dropped the glass she was holding. Her father was directly behind her, skin gray and black-veined. She saw the bite mark on his arm.

"Daddy?"

Nicholas had turned. Momma must've bitten him earlier. He ran out of the room so fast she figured he just needed some time alone to process Momma's death. Shay didn't think about him getting bit.

Nicholas reached for Shay; his grasp uncannily strong as he gripped her shoulder. Shay struggled, tried her best to push him away but his hand wouldn't release her. She stumbled, reached back, and grabbed the knife off the counter that she'd used to cut lemons with.

"Don't make me do it," Shay said.

Nicholas's teeth were cracking like a snapping turtle. He leaned closer. She stabbed him in the neck. The wound didn't stop him. Shay's veins lit with panic. She had to fight. She couldn't die like this. Shay's heart was pounding. She wouldn't die like this. She stabbed her father over and over but nothing stopped him. He still pushed and grabbed and tried to bite her. Then Shay remembered the head. She positioned her knife and slammed it into the side of her father's skull.

———

Jed wasn't sure he could eat, but the sun had risen and they'd missed breakfast. He thought of coffee and decided against it. He held out a trembling hand. The caffeine would make him shake more. He needed steady hands.

Breaking glass echoed. Jed stood, weary on his feet, and walked through the kitchen door.

Shay jabbed a knife into the side of Nicholas's skull. The large man dropped to the ground like a sack of shit.

Shay was covered in blood. She tore at her clothes, wiping at her skin, grabbing a towel off the counter and rubbing her arms so she could see. Terrified and hyperventilating, she was looking for bite marks.

"Check my back," she yelled at Jed. "Am I bit?" She was in full panic mode. "I don't know what happened." Her hands flitted across her neck, she twisted her hair up and checked behind her ears.

"You're okay." Jed picked her up and took her to the bathroom. "I'll look you over. It's going to be all right." Shay was a feather in his arms, warm and soft, and he wanted to hold her forever until she settled.

He released her legs and set her on her feet.

Jed turned on the shower and pushed Shay inside. From the entrance, he turned Shay, spraying her skin with the handheld piece of the shower. He checked beneath her clothes; her shoulders, wrists and arms, the soft skin of her neck. "You're good." He handed the shower head to her. "I'll be back in a few minutes. Don't leave this room until I come back."

Shay nodded.

Jed used the floating spell to get Nicholas and Momma to the burn pile. He didn't even leave the grounds of the ranch, couldn't imagine making one more trip there today. He sent sparks to the new bodies, ensuring they burned. Thick, black smoke rose into the sky. He was grateful the ranch was far enough away that the smell wasn't too strong.

Shay was still in the shower, crying–no–sobbing like he'd never heard before. That was wrong, she sobbed just as hard as Jed wished he could have the night his own mother died. They were bound by that trauma now.

He searched the kitchen drawers until he found a Sharpie. Then he went to work. Each doorway was etched with protection runes. He found a stock of salt in the cupboard and lined the doorways and windows. Then he went upstairs and did the same to Shay's room.

They needed to leave, but not tonight. First thing in the morning he'd convince her. Too much had happened here, and he was way behind on getting to California.

CHAPTER 25

SHAY SAT ON THE FLOOR OF THE SHOWER LONG after the water had turned cold. She sobbed, forehead resting on her knees, arms hanging at her sides. She felt empty. Alone. So much had happened in such a short time. So many people's lives had been affected; Shay told herself that there was no way she could avoid it all. The safety of the ranch was nothing more than a fairytale, a dream, a lie. It couldn't protect her. Her parents couldn't protect her.

Shay wondered if she'd never ran off to that dive bar and met Clyburn, maybe he'd never have found the ranch. This was all her fault. There were too many connecting points. She should have been a better daughter. She should have simply accepted that she wasn't going to college during the apocalypse instead of running off for one last night of freedom. It wasn't even worth what she'd gone through. Those few minutes with a handsome cowboy in a dive bar parking lot were definitely not worth losing everything.

Shay hated herself.

The water suddenly turned off.

"Come on." Jed's voice broke her concentration.

Shay looked up. Jed was holding open a towel. She wasn't one to walk around naked, but Shay suddenly didn't care anymore. There was no one; she was alone.

"It's gonna be okay." Jed tucked the towel under his chin, reached down, and pulled up Shay by her arms. He wrapped the towel around her shaking body and led her out of the shower. They walked down the hall, up the stairs, and stopped in Shay's room.

Her room smelled strange, like lavender and bergamot and thyme. There were candles lit with etchings. A bundle of sage was smoking in the corner. There were marks over her windows and doors, all over the moldings and floors.

"What happened in here?"

"Spells of protection." Jed rubbed her with the towel to dry her. His eyes searched her skin, closer this time.

"Do you see any teeth marks?"

"No." Jed's gaze stopped at her lips.

Shay was reminded of that feeling she had when she saw Jed for the first time in the Lame Deer casino. Something bloomed deep inside her stomach and tingled like a butterfly. She was experiencing it again.

Jed moved, just a quarter of an inch closer. His eyes searched her face. Shay knew she'd been through a lot today. She didn't want to think about all of that. She wanted to focus on the mood, the warmth of Jed's hands on her arms, the feeling of safety in this room. Shay reached up on her toes and kissed him.

Jed was gentle. His hands skimmed over her body, his lips brushed against hers. Shay wondered if he felt the same explosion as she did.

He pushed her backward, toward the bed. When her legs hit the mattress, he bent to pull the blankets back.

"Lay down." He was still so close. His breath moved her hair.

Shay sat and scooted back. Jed reached for the blankets again and pulled them over her. He tucked her in and kissed her forehead. "Sleep," he said.

Shay suddenly couldn't keep her eyes open. For an instant, she thought maybe she should panic or fear whatever he'd done to her and the room. But she couldn't. There was nothing left inside her to care if she lived or died. She had nothing. Her world had shifted so drastically that she welcomed the void of sleep and didn't care if she never woke.

CHAPTER 26

Jed could barely keep up with Declan. Hooves threw up dirt as the horses ran full gallop. Light from the full moon reflected off the sandy beach. In the distance, there was a boat waiting for them.

"Don't look back." Declan was out of breath. He'd been chanting spells and throwing bolts of energy at the mass of beasts that were hot on their tail.

Jed looked back, wishing instantly that he hadn't. A black cloud was following them. Animalistic growls and claws made Jed's heart tick faster. The thing was a demon like they'd never seen before.

"I said don't do that!" Declan shouted. Sweat poured down the man's face. They'd barely made it out of the little house in Chesapeake City. The clapboard building they'd called home for two years was currently burning to cinder. White smoke rose in the distance, and both knew the fire had spread. By morning, half of Chesapeake City would be ash because of them, because they were scorned men in the right place at the right time. Jed wanted to leave after the beast had killed Eileen, but Declan was adamant that their runes and spells of protection were solid.

———

They *were* solid. For a few weeks at least, until the simple push of a broom knocked over a chair, then a glass of water. The water washed away a perfectly placed line of salt, which melted away etchings of chalk and coal. The Demon found them before Declan could pull chalk out of his pocket and fix it. Jed had been wringing out a cloth to soak up the water before it could spread farther and cause more damage. The blast through the wall threw Jed into a table. Declan was crouched on the floor and shielded his head.

The roar was deafening.

Jed shoved clapboard off his body and scrambled to his feet. Dust and smoke filled the room.

"Run boy!" Declan shouted. "I'll take care of it."

Jed flashed back to a time when he was much younger, when he knew just enough, when his mother shoved him out of a moving train car near Boston. "Run!" her voice was hushed and anguished. Jed had rolled down an embankment. He stopped and looked up just in time to see her closing the train car door, trapping herself inside with the Angel who'd found them. He couldn't leave Declan. He was older now, stronger; he could do *something*.

Jed tapped his fingers together in spellcasting, he knew better than parlor tricks now. He spat words that sounded like potatoes frying, his fingers twisted like a ballerina's legs, and he shot bolts of electricity at the angry cloud. Striking a taloned foot, the creature roared and advanced.

"I told ye to go!" Declan's accent was starting to show through.

The men cast barriers, shocks, water, threw pieces of the table. Nothing worked. Jed noticed the creature strayed from the woodstove. He changed direction, ripped open the door of the woodstove and used a spell to hurdle the burning coals at the monster. It howled as the coals left holes in its clouded body.

"Yes!" Declan copied Jed and they began hurdling the fire together. The coals dropped to the floor and within minutes the monster was as porous as Swiss cheese, but the wooden floor of the house was smoking. The clapboard house was the best tinder fire had ever met. The hot coals quickly took root against the floorboards and lit a flame that grew as tall as a man.

The fire kept the creature at bay while Declan and Jed grabbed a few necessities and ran.

They didn't get far before the creature was following them. Jed tried to cast invisibility glamour, but he hadn't perfected it and their images glitched and wavered like ghosts as they ran down Pig Alley and turned at Harry Jackson Street.

"The canal," Declan said. "We can lose it in the water."

Jed pointed to the two horses tethered at a shop. "Or outrun it. The boat is at Hack Point."

"I like your thinking, boy." Declan veered toward the horses and Jed followed.

The cloud had multiplied as they galloped over the bridge. Two taloned legs became four, then eight, then twelve. Jaws with rows of sharp teeth snapped and hissed. Jed didn't count how many. He told himself he wasn't going to look back again. He slapped the horse on its flank so it would gallop faster.

The boat was close.

"I'll cut the dock lines," Declan said. The blade of a hunting knife glinted moonlight. "You start the engine."

It sounded easy enough. Jed threw blasts of fire over his shoulder to distract the Demon that was coming for them. Sweat dripped into his eyes. Panic filled his chest. They were so close.

The horse slowed on the dock, unused to the wavering motion. "Ha," Jed slapped the horse, but it reared up. Jed slid off, glanced at Declan, and leapt onto the boat. He made a mad dash for the engine room, felt stupid when he looked for keys before using his luck to turn over the engine. He didn't even have to whisper the words of a spell, the magic came out of him naturally. The boat engine sputtered to life.

Declan wasn't on the deck.

Jed ran from the engine room, gripped the deck railing, and found him. Declan was warding off the beast with the hunting knife and a fistful of fire. Neither seemed to be working against the beast.

"Be gone with ya!" He shouted at the Demon.

The mass roared and snapped, its cloudlike body undulated and twisted like a tornado. Thunderclap reverberated and drowned out Declan's voice.

Jed raised both hands and threw fire. "Run!" He shouted to Declan.

Declan rounded the dock and ran for the boat. "Hit the gas!"

Jed walked backward, but to get to the gas he'd have to

stop throwing the fire. He shook his hands, dashed toward the gears, and accelerated. He ran back to the deck.

The boat was moving away from the dock, Declan was running full bore. Jed held out a hand and steadied himself.

Declan leapt, stopping midair as wicked jaws clamped down on his leg with a sickening crunch.

"No!" Jed screamed into the night.

Jed would never forget the look on Declan's face. The man smiled as his body hit the wooden dock. "I knew it would come one day." Declan's fingers tapped together and made a strange motion before the black cloud of teeth and talons consumed him.

Jed felt a bulge in his pocket as Declan vanished. He reached for it and pulled out Declan's spell book.

Jed was filled with anguish and hate as he strode to the engine room, pushed the boat into high gear, and set toward Elk River then the Atlantic.

CHAPTER 27

Jed watched the sky from the bedroom window. There had been too much commotion. Four Demons escaping Hell would get around. The chatter between Heaven, Hell, and the Earthen plane would mention him. He didn't need more heat. Jed needed to get moving.

"We have to go," Jed said as Shay opened her eyes.

"I know."

She looked tired. She'd barely moved all night after he settled in the bed and curled around her, his arm wrapped tight across her stomach.

She smelled like leather and lavender. Jed didn't want to forget it as he buried his nose in her braid and breathed in.

Shay's fingers traced his.

Jed stopped. This was dangerous. He moved away, rolled, and stood on the opposite side of the bed. He began collecting the things he'd left around her room. The sage, a white feather, small pouches that held spells.

"Yesterday..." Shay started. "What happened?"

"Seems your buddy Clyburn made a deal with a crossroads Demon and it came to collect." Jed opened Shay's closet and took out a backpack.

"What are you doing?" Shay asked.

"Helping you pack." Jed threw the pack into a nearby chair.

"I'm already packed."

Jed glanced around the room for another bag.

"It's downstairs. We have bugout bags ready to go. I don't need anything from in here." Shay moved to her feet, dragging the blanket to cover herself.

She was showing a lot of skin and Jed wanted to touch her, more than he had during the night. But that would take time, and they didn't have time for touching each other in a dark room.

Shay opened a dresser drawer and took out clothes. She dropped the blanket to dress and Jed turned around rather than watch like a creeper.

"We gotta go, Shay." Jed's voice was low. He wanted to stay here with her, alone and safe to play house. But *they* would come soon enough.

Shay nodded and headed for the door to her bedroom. Jed followed her downstairs and into the kitchen. Shay opened a closet and removed a large backpack.

"You want one?" she asked. "You could take Daddy's pack."

"Sure." Jed wasn't going to say no to supplies.

"We should just bring them all. Can't hurt." Shay pulled out two more bags. "We can get some food from the root cellar if you want." She removed the guns next and tucked a small, black handgun into her holster.

Jed stepped over the blood stain on the floor, grabbed two of the packs, and opened the door to the porch. "We should go now, before they find me next."

Shay followed. "We can take the Jeep." She grabbed keys hanging near the door and pressed a button on the key fob. "Why so urgent?" she asked, opening a drawer filled with ammo and emptying it into her bag.

"I'm being hunted. Every moment of my life. We can't stay here. Angels or Demons will come to find me." He threw the bags into the back of the Jeep Commander that was parked near the house.

"But why are they after you?" Shay asked.

"I'm forbidden; the product of an Archangel and a human woman. Most infants are killed at birth. I seem to have lasted a bit longer." A strange feeling warred inside Jed. He'd never told a human what he was, always skirted around the issue.

"I can't leave yet," Shay said as she began walking toward the horse barn.

Chapter 28

Nero was still alive, kicking and whinnying and not happy about being locked up while the ranch was overrun and destroyed.

"I know," Shay said as she unlatched the gate to his stall.

"We can't take him," Jed warned.

Shay nodded, emptiness in her heart. Nero was the last of her family. She opened the bin of food and got fresh water from the spigot. "I can't leave him trapped on the ranch."

"That wouldn't be humane." Jed stood near the door, watching the long path to the gates of the ranch.

Shay could tell he wanted to go. Now. She couldn't leave Nero to starve to death. She removed his blanket and brushed his back one last time. "We have to go, Nero. This man is going to keep me safe." She glanced up. "Or maybe I'm going to keep him safe. Seems we're both a bit of a mess right now. Either way, you can't come with us."

Nero neighed and shook his head as though he understood every word Shay said.

"You can't stay here either." Shay moved to the door. "Come on, boy."

The three walked past the gardens and empty chicken coop splashed with blood.

Shay passed Jed the keys and walked Nero to the gate.

Nero huffed, looking between the ranch and the open Montana prairie in front of them.

Shay stroked his neck. "Stay away from the roads. Stay away from those smelly walking corpses. Stick to the mountains." Nero nuzzled her. "You'll find the wild horses. I know you will." Shay's eyes were filled with tears as Jed pulled up next to her. "You'll forget me but I'll never forget you."

She got in the Jeep. Nero watched her with wide eyes, huffing and pawing at the ground.

Shay rolled down the window. "Go now, Nero." She waved him away and broke down.

Jed pulled away, leaving the horse alone at the open gate. Shay felt a warm hand on her leg, a squeeze. She cried harder. Jed accelerated and Shay watched the road in front of them with blurry vision. After a few minutes, there was a black blur in her periphery. She turned. Nero was running next to the Jeep, his black mane flowing in the wind. The Jeep accelerated. Nero tipped his head down, determined, and ran faster, keeping up with them.

"I can't do this," Shay cried, reaching a hand out the window. Nero was too far away, but he saw her and he ran faster, trying to keep up.

Jed squeezed her leg again before putting both hands on the steering wheel and accelerating to well over a hundred miles per hour. Nero couldn't keep up. Shay couldn't watch him give up on her.

Chapter 29

Jed kept his eyes on the road. He didn't want to hit debris or an errant dead person walking across the road. Shay was wiping her face with her shirt and trying to put herself back together.

"I'm sorry," Jed said, swerving around an upside-down car.

"It's not your fault." She took a deep breath. "I've had Nero since I was a little girl. I never thought I'd have to let him go."

"We can't hold on to everything."

"I know." Shay's voice was quiet. She kept leaning forward to look at the side view mirror to see if the horse was following.

"Take thirty-nine to Rosebud Cut-off Road. That will avoid Lame Deer." Shay buckled her seatbelt and leaned back in the seat.

"Will it avoid the Cheyenne lands?" Jed asked.

"Until we get to route 212. Then Cheyenne lands border the south."

Jed nodded, his lips pressed together in thought. He didn't want to run in to the Crow men again. He had enough shit to deal with.

"I'm headed to California. There's someone there who can help me." Jed's voice was serious but hopeful.

"You sure this someone is still alive?"

"He can't really die."

Shay turned to stare at the side of Jed's face.

"I can bring you elsewhere. If that's what you want." He swallowed hard, gripped the steering wheel with both hands, and looked straight ahead. Sure he had magic and luck and his father's looks, but he still feared her rejection. She might have an aunt or an uncle in the next town over that she'd rather stay with.

"I've got no one else." Shay's voice was low. "Just you, Jed."

"It's gonna be dangerous." She might run away with what he was going to tell her next. "Things seem okay right now but they'll come for me. An Angel or a Demon. I think my friend in California can help."

"What's his name?"

"Sparrow."

"That's a bird not a man."

Jed shrugged. "He's kinda weird."

"Perfect. Zombies and Demons and Angels and weird men from California named after a little bird." Shay laughed. "The things I've learned since meeting you–" she glanced at her watch "–nearly 96 hours ago. You've changed my world in less than five business days."

"Sorry 'bout that."

Shay touched his arm and a feeling zipped straight to

his chest. He didn't want her to go, he didn't want her to meet Sparrow. He wanted nothing more than to drive her to a secluded place and never leave. But that wasn't possible. He hoped she could accept a life on the run.

"Stay with me, Jed." Shay rubbed his arm.

"What do you mean?"

"You went somewhere just now. You looked lost."

"I have been lost for a long time. But I think it will get better now that you're here. Why don't you get some rest?" Jed suggested.

"I'll try." Shay shifted in her seat, removing her hand from his arm.

Jed felt cold at the loss of her touch. He turned off Route 39. Glancing in the rear-view mirror he was almost certain he saw a black shadow in the woods.

———

Shay woke startled, the Jeep jerking to the right and accelerating.

"What's happening?" Her hand was on her holster as she sat up.

"Bumpy road," Jed was checking the windows and mirrors.

"Did you run over some corpses?"

"Avoided those." Jed chuckled.

The sun was setting over the mountains. There were craters in the road, like someone had thrown a stick of dynamite at a car or a body. Jed had to keep veering off the road so the Jeep wouldn't get stuck in one of the craters.

"That's ugly." Shay inspected the road.

"Do you want to stop up here and stretch your legs?" Jed asked. "We haven't passed a town in a while and the roadsigns said Big Sky is fifteen miles away.

"Big Sky is nice." Shay stretched and the hem of her shirt rode up, revealing skin. "I could eat. And we're going to need gas." Shay turned her attention to watching the pine trees that they passed.

"What's wrong?" Jed asked.

"I feel guilty." Shay touched her face. "It's all my fault."

"What happened at the ranch is not your fault."

Shay made a noise deep in her throat; it sounded like a strangled cry she was holding down. "I brought Clyburn. I ran away one night because I didn't want to stay at the ranch, I wanted to go to college with my friends." She took a deep breath in the middle of her confession. "I met Clyburn at a bar. Things happened. Then a few days later he showed up at the ranch."

"That explains his obsession with you." Jed was making a face like he'd sucked salt.

"What I'm trying to say is that if I'd never run off that night, he'd have never entered our lives. My parents are dead because of me. The ranch is gone because of me." Shay was crying again. Quietly. Tears streamed down her face.

Jed slowed the Jeep and pulled over. The roads were empty and he hadn't seen a soul in miles. He turned off the engine and got out, rounding the Jeep and opening the passenger door.

"What are you doing?" Shay asked as she wiped her face.

Jed moved her whole body so she was sitting sideways,

facing him. He stood between her legs. "I can make it go away. If you don't want to remember."

"What do you mean?" Shay was shocked at the way he went to her side.

Jed touched her forehead. Calloused fingers causing her skin to tingle and heat. "Like I made this go away." His eyes searched hers. Shay saw pain there. Pain just as bad as hers and somehow he'd kept going all this time. "I can rid you of those memories."

Shay shook her head. "No. I hate myself for ever meeting Clyburn. But I can't forget. If I forget and I make that mistake again. I can't…" her gaze drifted away from his face until she was focused off in the distance.

Jed gripped her chin and forced her to look at him. "You will never make that mistake again." Jed leaned closer, his lips brushing hers. "Because I am here and no one else will be touching you ever again." His lips pressed against hers, harder.

Shay reached for him, her hands sliding over the hard planes of his stomach, his sides, around to his back. Jed leaned into her. Shay wanted to touch more of him. She gripped his shirt, wanting to feel the skin under his clothing. She wanted him to quell the ache in her center and was out of breath in a few minutes.

Jed pulled away. "We have to keep going." His face was pained; he tugged her hips closer and she didn't miss his hardness pressed against her center.

Shay hid her disappointment. "Yeah. We should go."

Jed swept a piece of hair off her cheek. "If you change your mind. Let me know." He was looking into her eyes intently.

"I won't change my mind." Shay moved in her seat as Jed closed the door and went to the driver's side of the Jeep.

———

They stopped at an abandoned gas station. Jed used his magic to make the gas pump work and topped off the Jeep. Shay had warned him that the road ahead was mountainous and few gas stations existed in the winding roadway. They had and extra tank, but it was better to be safe than sorry.

"See if the television works," Jed said to Shay as she went to investigate the shop.

"You watch T.V.?"

"Just the news, lately. There's a horde moving through California that I've been tracking." Jed's fingers twisted and tapped and the gas pump came to life.

He watched Shay as she went inside. They'd planned to make a few of the camp meals in the bugout bags but Shay didn't want to use up all the water. Just in case, she'd said.

He saw the blue light of the television turning on, static as she flipped the channels. The gas pump turned off when the tank was full. Jed secured it and went inside.

"Anything?" he asked.

"Not yet." She kept pressing the button on the television until a map displayed on the screen.

"Wait," Jed said. He moved closer. More of California was designated a red zone. There were no newscasters on this channel, just a display of the U.S. red zones and green zones. There were little army man clusters for where the National Guard was stationed.

"You want to go to California?" Shay asked. "Still? It looks like a bad idea."

Jed made a noise. "To some. But Sparrow is there. I'm sure of it. And he's going to keep us safe until this mess is over."

Jed turned, focused out the window. He was sure he saw a shadow out of his periphery. Shadows were never good. The veil between realms was thinning with whatever was going on with the dead walking. The four Demons at the ranch would have brought consequences and Angels, and he'd seen none yet. Whatever shadow he'd seen wouldn't be good, and it had been twice now. They needed to disappear.

"We should go," Jed said.

"Waters." Shay pointed to a package of bottled water on a shelf.

"Let's eat later," he suggested, feeling unease and something in the air.

Shay grabbed a few packs of jerky and tucked them under her arm. They each grabbed a pack of water and headed to the Jeep. Jed opened the cargo door.

"Why the rush?" Shay asked.

"I want to beat the California horde before it gets too far north." He didn't want to tell her about the shadow. He didn't want to scare her. It could simply be a bear or an elk or a passerby in the thinning veil between realms. Hell was simply a reflection of the Earthen plane after all.

CHAPTER 30

T HERE WAS A DARK SKY, THE MILKY WAY BRIGHT
like it had never been before. Shay was leaned forward
watching the stars out the front window.

"Look," she pointed at a falling star.

Something twisted in Jed's gut. Falling stars were interesting to those who didn't know what they could be. Sometimes it was more than a star; sometimes it was an Angel
being cast out or dropping in to the Earthen plane to cause
havoc.

"That's cool." Jed focused on the dark road in front of
them as he descended the winding foothills. The route had
become more cluttered with debris in the road; fallen trees
and broken-down cars. It hadn't taken long for the roads to
crumble into potholes as the veil between realms thinned
and the Earthen plane darkened. There was an ochre cast to
the sun and the moon, the shadows darker than they'd ever
been before. Jed took in the changes on the Earthen plane
and hoped finding Sparrow would set things back to the
way they belonged.

"You want something to eat?" Shay was reaching behind the seat for one of the bugout bags.

"Nah." Jed leaned toward the window, relaxing. "I'll wait. If I start eating now I won't want to stop."

"You one of those people who eats every meal like it could be their last?" Shay was joking but a little serious.

The ground shook, vibrating the Jeep.

"What was that?" Shay asked.

A figure came into focus in the headlights.

"Fuck." Jed hit the brakes.

Shay gripped the door and braced herself for impact. "You're going to hit it."

"Probably not." Jed knew what it was and how fast it would move. He reached for his bag that was on the floor behind his seat. Fingers searching, he felt the worn fabric of it but couldn't get a good grip.

Jed slammed on the brakes. The Jeep came to a stop, inches from the figure. Jed finally grabbed the bag.

The figure sneered.

"Oh my God." Shay covered her mouth. "Is that?" She couldn't turn away from the giant winged man in the road. "Is that an Angel?"

"Nasty bastards." Jed pulled a knife from his bag. "He shouldn't have his wings out like that. Kinda uncouth."

"I don't see wings," Shay said, eyes wide.

"You can't?"

Shay shook her head. "Maybe just you can?"

The Angel jumped onto the hood of the Jeep and ripped the corner of the roof off, throwing it to the side. He looked at Shay and smiled darkly. Nothing good could come from a face so handsome and a smile so devilish.

"Not today." Jed's fingers danced with a spell. He spat words that sounded like hate laced with ice, and he shot an electric current at the Angel.

The Angel stumbled back two steps and redirected his focus to Jed. He lurched forward and reached into the Jeep, grabbing Jed by the arms and dragging him out.

"Run!" Jed warned Shay just before the Angel took him to the sky. "Get out of here!"

"No!" Shay shouted.

Shay scrambled into the driver's seat, slammed the vehicle into drive and sped down the road after the two men.

She swerved around debris, trying to focus on the figures in the sky. When the road was clear, she grabbed the handgun from her holster and aimed.

The Angel and Jed were fighting in the sky. Shay couldn't shoot; they were moving too fast. She sped up, hoping to get a better aim.

As the Angel threw Jed, sparks and fire flitted from Jed's hands. Shay could hear their voices faintly as they fought.

Jed fell. He had to be a few stories up in the air. The Angel flung Jed by the arms and he dropped. Shay sped up, reaching out the top of the Jeep and aiming at the Angel. She fired off a few shots, glad that she'd missed as the Angel grabbed Jed just before he hit the ground. Jed swiped at the Angel with a knife.

Suddenly, the Jeep hit something. Shay focused on the road, weaving around large tree branches. She glanced between the figures fighting in the sky and the road which had become covered in branches. Not far ahead of her, there was a giant tree that had fallen across the road. End to end, there was no way around it. Shay cursed. She slowed as she got closer and tried to drive over it but the tires just tore apart the rotting bark. Shay got out. She took one look at the road and Jed in the distance and screamed in frustration. She was going to lose everyone and could do nothing about it. Defeat swelled in her chest. Shay didn't want it all to end like this. She wasn't about to run away like a coward but she didn't want to die at the hands of that Angel once it was done with Jed.

"Goddamn it!" Shay kicked the tree that was blocking the road.

Behind Shay, a familiar noise broke through the night; the sound of galloping hooves on rough pavement. Shay turned, barely believing the sight. Nero was running toward her at full gallop.

"Nero!" Shay scrambled and climbed up on to the hood of the Jeep. "Come here. Good boy." Shay jumped onto Nero's back as he passed. Landing hard, she gripped his mane and held on tight as the horse leapt over the fallen trees. "Keep going, boy. We gotta get to Jed."

Shay focused ahead. The men were still fighting, closer to the ground now. Shay saw a chance. She aimed and fired twice.

The Angel roared as a bullet hit its shoulder. Jed dropped and grabbed onto the Angel's leg.

Shay shot it in the wing as she urged Nero to move faster. The Angel dropped as one wing weakened its ability to fly.

Nero slowed. Shay saw her chance. The Angel was holding onto Jed with one arm, punching him. Shay shot the Angel in the arm. Blood and bone sprayed as her bullet hit bone. The Angel dropped Jed but they were closer to the ground. He fell hard, shouting as his legs buckled. He didn't get up.

Shay swung her leg and jumped off Nero. She shot the Angel again, running hard until she came upon Jed. The Angel fell to the ground. Shay stole the knife from Jed's hand, leapt over his body. In a few quick strides she was at the Angel's body. She paused, but knew she shouldn't have. She'd never gazed upon a man so beautiful before. Muscled and smooth skin, the man looked as though he had been chiseled from stone. The Angel's eyes flashed open. Shay slammed the knife into its chest. The Angel never took another breath; his body went limp, lifeless.

Shay stood slowly, weary, unbelieving.

Nero huffed, drawing Shay's attention. When she turned around, the horse was nuzzling Jed's still body.

A lump was rising in Shay's throat. She didn't see the whole fight, but what she did see was brutal.

Shay crouched near Jed noticing how pale his little bit of untattooed skin looked in the moonlight. Blood dripped out of his mouth. There were cuts all over his body. At least he was breathing faintly.

"Hey," she said as she shook his shoulder. She checked the pulse in his neck. It was weak but there. "What am I gonna do with you?" she muttered as she took in their surroundings.

Shay considered herself strong, but Jed was twice her size. They were sitting ducks in the road; there was no protection from the elements or the dead or an attack from an ethereal creature. Shay needed to get him back to the

Jeep. She knew there was a tarp and rope in the cargo area. She glanced at the Jeep that was a few hundred yards away, then she glanced at Nero.

"You stay with him," she told Nero as she jogged to the Jeep.

Shay opened the cargo hatch. Everything was stored neatly and had been inventoried weekly at the ranch. Nicholas wanted everything ready to go in case they had to run. Emotion welled in Shay's chest. She never thought she'd be running without her parents at her side. She grabbed the heavy duty tarp and the paracord rope, then went back to where Jed was laying in the road.

Shay unfolded the tarp and set it out next to Jed. She lifted and shoved his body, pushing the tarp under one side of him, then pulling it out on the opposite side until he was centered. She used the paracord to fashion a harness of sorts around Nero's shoulders and back, then tied through the eyelets in the tarp.

"Let's do this, boy." Shay patted Nero, her arms burning from exertion, and led him toward the Jeep as he dragged Jed's body. They wove around the downed trees until they got to the giant one that was blocking the entire road.

"We have to go over it," Shay told Nero. She gripped the back of the tarp and lifted. "Slowly, boy."

Nero stepped over the tree trunk, dragging Jed over. Shay's arms ached as she lifted her side and did her best to make sure his head didn't hit the road.

Getting his body into the back of the Jeep was going to take a lot more effort. Shay put the seats down and laid out a wool blanket. She released Nero from the rope, wound it up and stored it. Shay tugged Jed closer and lifted him under his arms.

The man was dead weight. A lot of dead weight. Nero bit at Jed's shirt and tugged up to help.

"Thanks boy, but I think we're going to need more than that."

Shay got him into a sitting position and tried lifting Jed from under his arms. Her muscles ached and back ached. "Jesus christ," she muttered. "Why is he so big?"

Nero huffed and walked to the driver's side door, tapping it with his nose.

"You can't drive." She looked at the coil of rope, then the tarp and where Nero was standing. "You know, Nero, you're a genius."

Shay used the rope and tied a harness to Nero again, then she fed the rope through the driver's side window, through the Jeep and out the back cargo door. She tied the rope through the eyelets again.

"Okay, boy," Shay said as she picked up the end of the tarp and clucked her tongue. "Go."

Nero walked forward, tugging the ropes and the tarp. Shay lifted the opposite end and they got Jed into the cargo area without much damage. He maybe had a few extra bruises, but it was better than leaving him in the road.

Before leaving, Shay returned to the dead Angel only to find that his body had turned to ash. The knife was still there. Shay knew it was special because of the carvings in the handle. She collected the knife and brought it back to the Jeep.

Shay checked on Jed one last time before closing the

hatch and getting behind the wheel. She kept the window down so she could talk to Nero.

"Gotta tuck away somewhere safe," she said as she reversed then turned around and drove from where they came.

Shay drove a good ten miles before she found a dead end road with a chain across a driveway. She let herself in and found an abandoned shack past a long driveway of thick trees. It looked like someone's hunting cabin and she figured it was safe enough. They were off the road and there was a stream nearby. Best of all, they weren't on Cheyenne land and she didn't have to worry about Hosa surprising them with the intention of skinning Jed.

Nero followed the Jeep, but eventually wandered off. Shay didn't try to stop him. She had a feeling he'd be nearby. She'd never been happier than the moment he broke through the darkness to help her.

Shay parked the Jeep under a large oak tree and turned off the engine before climbing in the back to check on Jed. She pressed her fingers to his neck. His pulse was good. She opened one of the bugout bags and got the first-aid kit.

Jed's clothes were torn, bloody, and dirty. She pushed the cloth away to inspect one of his wounds before deciding the clothes were going to have to go. She took the scissors out of the kit and began cutting his shirt away at the neck. Shay had never seen so many tattoos. They covered his chest and stomach. The more of his shirt that she cut, the more she saw. They weren't pictures but strange shapes and markings like what he'd carved into her bedroom doorframe.

A mosquito buzzed in her ear. Shay swatted at the bug

and glanced at the ripped open roof of the Jeep. She needed to patch it or the mosquitoes would eat them alive in the night. Shay left Jed's side, took one of the rescue blankets and tucked it around the frame. It wouldn't last, but it would work for tonight.

Shay crawled to Jed's side again. She found a fresh cloth in the bag and used a bottle of water to clean his wounds. Some were shallow scrapes but a few were deep and still bleeding. Shay watched his face as she cleaned the worst of the cuts, a large slash over his abdomen. He didn't flinch or moan. She wasn't sure if that was a good thing or bad at the moment. She didn't need him howling in pain but she did need to know he had some life left in him.

Shay considered a pressure dressing, but when the wound kept oozing bright red blood, she decided suturing would be better. Thankfully momma and Shay had packed the med kit with everything they could need for wound care: Lidocaine spray, sutures, sterile gauze, and needles.

Shay set out her supplies and got to work. When she was finished stitching, the sun was fading fast. Shay made quick work of putting a sterile dressing over the fresh stitches before finding a camp light.

Her back and legs ached from being hunched over in the Jeep. She searched for the battery powered lantern, found it under the seat and clicked it on. Shay's gaze drifted over Jed's body. She still had to get his pants off. She reached for his belt, unbuckling the leather and pulling. She rolled it up and set it aside. Next she unsnapped his jeans, set the scissors just below the zipper, and began cutting. She tried not to stare at the corded muscles or trail of hair below his abdomen that tucked below the black band of his boxer-briefs. She assessed the cuts on his legs and bruising as she worked. After the jeans were cut and removed, she took his boots and socks off. She washed the dirt off his legs and used an ACE bandage to wrap his swollen right ankle. She'd seen his legs buckle when he fell and she was thankful it wasn't a break.

Shay still had to check his back. The tarp protected him from dragging wounds but she'd seen him fall and get tossed through the air like a ragdoll. As Shay moved closer, settling her knees against his side, she gripped his shoulder and hip. She rocked his limp body once, twice, and on the third time she rolled him. Nicholas had taught her how to move and carry the fainting goats or lifeless sheep in similar fashion. But Jed was much larger than a farm animal. She wasn't sure where she found the strength to move him. She pulled it from somewhere deep inside.

Shay tipped the lantern closer and inspected his back. There were fewer tattoos along his shoulder blades and spinal column, the rest was bare. Shay's fingers roamed over his skin, checking small cuts and palpating for bleeding. She'd read in one of the survival books that if the liver was injured there could be pain in the abdomen or shoulder. Jed didn't budge when she pressed her fingers into his muscle. She settled him back and tucked a spare blanket under his head to use as a pillow.

Shay found another blanket to cover Jed before she climbed into the driver's seat and turned on the headlights. She needed to stretch her legs and use the bathroom but didn't want any surprises. The night was quiet; she couldn't hear anything more than the rippling stream, the chirping of crickets and the echo of a barn owl. Across the stream

Shay saw two eyes watching her. She recognized the form. It was Nero, settled down for the night. "Hey, boy," she whispered, happy that he was nearby.

Shay cleaned herself up, drank a bottle of water, and ate a protein bar before taking off her boots and climbing in the back of the Jeep again. She was bone tired. The fight with the Angel had amped up her adrenaline and now she was coming down off the high. Shay was thankful for all her parents had taught her on the ranch. If she hadn't spent her life riding horses and hunting and being pushed to survive, she wasn't sure how this day would have ended.

She settled near Jed, then decided to move closer when the chill in the air made her shiver. It was cold outside as a Montana winter was getting closer. The windows in the jeep fogged. Shay turned off the lantern and focused on the sound of Jed's shallow breathing. She hoped he'd wake up soon and infection wouldn't set in. She guessed he probably had some more broken ribs too but she couldn't tell with the tattoos that covered his body. They hid the bruises and scrapes. In better light she'd examine him further.

Shay closed her eyes, reached out and took Jed's hand, fingers threaded together in a prayer. She prayed she didn't dream of that Angel she'd killed. He was both beautiful and fearsome and somehow she'd found the strength to end his life. Her daddy would've been proud had he been alive to see it. Shay sighed and scooted closer until their shoulders touched and fell fast asleep.

———

THE WARM BODY next to Shay was both a comfort and a pleasure. She propped herself up on an elbow and watched Jed. Some color had returned to his face and his breathing wasn't as shallow. She checked the pulse in his wrist and concluded with the steady beat that he was better than last night. She pulled the blanket back and checked the dressing over his stitched abdomen. There was some oozing, but it wasn't bad. She'd seen worse living on a ranch; wounds that the ranch hands had hidden and let fester because they were too proud for medical care.

Shay pulled the blanket back further. Jed's skin prickled to gooseflesh with the chill. In the morning sun, Shay got an even better view of his body. There were deep bruises around his ribs and as she traced them with her finger, she felt the unmistakable bulge of a break. She tested it, pressing harder. Jed groaned, his face twisting. She moved on, tracing his other ribs and found a few healed notches. There were scars she came across as well, a deep scar with bad stitches under his bicep. Battlefield medicine. That's what it looked like. Jed had probably never seen a real doctor for any of his ailments.

She tipped his head to the side and noticed a small scar on his neck. Two holes. A bitemark from something. She stared at his relaxed face as the sun shone through the Jeep's windows. He was beyond handsome and Shay figured his kind were forbidden because they'd take all the human women. Shay wasn't sure she would ever find another man attractive after looking at Jed.

Shay took her bugout bag and Jed's torn clothing. She got out of the Jeep and made her way to the stream that was a few feet away. There was frost on the tall grass and the fresh scent of cold air. Nero was gone, probably off in the prairie looking for sweet grass.

Shay was thankful for the gently sloping watershed. She tore Jed's shirt into strips, then rinsed them out. She hung the strips on nearby tree branch to dry, saving one to wash herself. She took in the surrounding prairie to make sure she was alone and there were no wandering eyes or wandering dead in the vicinity. Then she stripped and stepped into the stream.

The water was ice-cold but the cloth smelled like Jed, sandalwood and musk and coffee. She scrubbed her skin until it was pink, removing the gore from the Angel battle and traces of Jed's blood.

Her hair was matted with dirt and sweat and blood. She laid down in the stream and let it rinse before scrubbing it with soap.

Air drying was more of a challenge in the Montana chill. She'd experienced colder while traveling with her father on a cattle drive. Although, there was much less fighting, blood, and death involved. She decided she could handle the chill if it was the worst inconvenience for the day.

Chapter 31

He should have died. Jed expelled all that magic fighting the Angel that he couldn't heal his own injuries. He could do nothing but sleep and heal slowly. Without Shay, he would've been a dead man. Jed owed Shay his life. He knew that the instant his eyes opened and he sensed her warmth near him.

He twisted to the side, sucking in a breath of pain. His entire body ached. His hand moved over his stomach and felt the rough edges of a bandage.

"Don't," Shay warned. "I can't heal your cuts like you did mine."

"The cuts are the least of my concern. I think a few ribs are broken." He righted himself, leaning on his elbow.

Jed touched Shay's cheek, his fingertips tracing her jaw, behind her ear, down her neck.

"Does it hurt?" she asked.

"Only because I can't do the things I want to do." His eyes were imploring, only focused on her.

"Don't pull your stitches." She warned. "I'm no Grand-mother Crow but I did practice on the ranch pig once."

Jed chuckled then winced. He laid back and took deep breaths. "Appropriate training." He touched her cheek with the back of his hand. "Your hair is wet."

"I took a bath."

He glanced at their surroundings. "There's a bathroom in here?" A smile tugged at the corner of his mouth. "Man this jeep is more spacious than I thought."

Shay pointed out the window and Jed saw the rippling stream. "Damn. I missed that?"

"The early bird gets the worm or the nudity." Shay moved. "I'll get some food. If you're up for eating something."

Jed grabbed the blanket that had pooled around his waist, prepared to throw it back, until he noticed he wasn't wearing much and it was quite cold without Shay next to him.

She was fully dressed.

"What happened to my clothes?" Jed rested his head on the makeshift pillow, feeling out of breath.

"I took them off you." Shay unzipped a bag and opened a bottle of water. "They're trashed." She pointed to the window to the strips of clothing drying in the tree.

"I'm not sure how I feel about being stripped naked while unconscious." Jed pulled the blanket up to his chest like a child hiding.

"Next time I'll do it while you're conscious." Shay smiled before returning to her task of preparing food. "There's a mark on your neck," Shay said, eyes watching him closely. "What is that from?"

Jed's hand flew to the small scars. "Ah..." He didn't want to tell her. "Something bit me once."

"Something?"

"Kind of like a vampire. But a person. Her name was Meg." Jed shook his head. "I'm not sure how to explain it to you but you'll understand when you meet Sparrow. He's different."

"Does Sparrow bite people in the neck also?" Shay handed him a water and a pack of protein chips.

"You could say that."

"Will he bite me in the neck? Should I be afraid?"

Possessiveness flooded Jed's body at the thought of Sparrow ever touching Shay. "If he touches you, I'll kill him." Jed didn't care if Sparrow was royalty from the Seven Kingdoms of Heaven, or Legion Commander of the Hellions. He'd send Sparrow's soul to another plane.

"Calm down, cowboy," Shay patted Jed's arm as she scooted closer to him with more food.

———

Climbing out of the Jeep was a challenge. Jed's ribs throbbed and the cut on his abdomen stretched against the stitches. Shay had given him a few hours of rest before she forced him to get outside. He felt relatively clean thanks to her scrubbing the grime off his body and tending to his wounds. He watched her now as he leaned against the Jeep, feeling weak and catching his breath. Shay was pulling a strip of cloth down from the tree branch for him. She found an empty bucket near the shed in the distance and set it in the water so he didn't have to stand or lay down in the stream.

"Let's go cowboy, the sun ain't waiting for you." Shay smiled and waved him over. She was strong and soft, barefoot in the creek, her jeans rolled up so they wouldn't get wet. Jed had a vision of children splashing in the water around them. He closed his eyes and remembered what he was. That was a future he could never have. It was dangerous enough bringing Shay along. He focused on her again as she was bent over, rinsing cloth in the water.

"It looks cold." Jed pushed against the Jeep until he was standing and cursed himself for missing the vision of her bathing naked in the sunrise. Need zipped down his spine and straight to his groin. Jed cursed and reminded himself he was wearing nothing but thin boxer-briefs and she'd definitely see what was on his mind if he didn't get his lust under control.

It was hard—not the walking, but the trying to ignore wanting her. After all, she had killed an Angel to save him, somehow gotten him to safety, and took care of him until he woke. She was strong, the strongest woman he'd ever met. Most would have left him there to die. But not Shay. Shay had determination in her bones and if he was the praying type, he'd thank God for her. But he never prayed, he learned that from Declan. Never pray to the God who forbade your existence and let all the planes relish in open season hunting your skin. Never.

Jed made it to the water, holding his breath when his bare feet met the cold stream. The chill felt good on his sore ankle but the rest of his body shivered.

"You can do it, big-boy," Shay joked as she held out her hand to steady him.

He moved past her and sat on the bucket. "You've dragged my hide through enough. Let me do it." Jed took a deep breath, flinching when his ribs flared with pain. It wasn't the first broken rib he endured, and he was sure it wouldn't be the last in his lifetime. He was certain a few more of his ribs were cracked and that's what made it so hard to breathe.

Shay passed Jed a wet cloth and the soap. "I'll get your back." She didn't give him a chance to reply. Instead she moved around him, pulled a cloth from the stream, and rinsed his back.

"Ah!" Jed's spine went straight as the cold water shocked his body.

Shay giggled as she rubbed the cloth with soap and went about scrubbing him with it. She was gentle around the bruises and cuts but scrubbed his neck with her bare hands. Jed leaned into her touch.

"Who did these tattoos on your back?" Shay asked.

"An old friend. Someone who was like me." The air changed and became uneasy; he wasn't ready to talk about Declan.

"Where is this friend?"

"Dead."

"I'm sorry about that."

Jed was thoughtful. Everyone he'd been close to had died. He worried about the same future for Shay. "Me too. He shouldn't have died."

She squeezed fresh water over his back to rinse. "Tip

your head back," she said. She wet his hair that was crusted with blood and massaged the strands and scalp.

A deep moan escaped Jed's lips.

"Wash your front, boy." Shay squeezed his head in deep massage.

"I can't." He was far too distracted by her fingertips pressing into his scalp. No one had ever touched him like this before.

"I won't be doing it." She rinsed his hair until the shaggy, light brown strands were clean and dripping. "That's better."

Jed took her wrist and dragged her around to face him, pulling her onto his lap.

Shay wasn't a prude. She could feel the evidence of his desire pressing against her hip. It flooded her body with warmth.

"What did I do to deserve you?" Jed's eyes were half-lidded as he focused on her mouth and tugged her closer. He'd never wanted anyone like this before, never trusted anyone with his secrets. He was prepared for a lifetime alone. He was wrong. He never knew how much he truly needed someone. That someone was Shay.

Chapter 32

Nero was bound to Shay from the moment she found him bucking and kicking at a bee nest during a cattle drive. He'd only been born a few hours earlier, dropped in the prairie grass by a mare who wasn't sure raising a foal in the offseason was such a good thing. When the bees came out of the ground and swarmed on her, she ran. She left him to die, wet and cold. But the warm Montana sun dried the wetness from his coat and mane, and he rose up on knobby-kneed legs only to be stung over and over again.

Shay wasn't much more than a teenager when she pointed to the black foal in the distance. It didn't take much to convince Nicholas to take the foal home. Shay lifted him, draping the small horse over her lap as she rode back to the ranch.

She bottle-fed him and carried him around like a baby. Two long legs over her shoulders and his hindquarters nearly tripping her. She tended to the stings on his soft belly and backside. She kept him in her room those first months until he was too big, then slept in the barn next to him every night until he was settled. That was all it took for Nero to tether himself to Shay. They were inseparable.

That night the crossroads Demons came, one entered the barn. It took goats and sheep. It got Nicholas's horse but when the Demon came upon the giant black stallion, he got nothing more than a scratch on Nero's hide before the horse kicked him so hard the Demon decided it wasn't worth fighting for that meal. Nero's coat was so black and glossy it reflected the moonlight and devoured it at the same time. The Demon was frightened of the creature. But that sometimes happens when evil creatures come across someone who has walked the line of life or death. The dance to live is halfway known, the dance to death is easy. Nero could kill just as the Demon.

Nero was still scratched. Long black claws didn't kill him, but they did change him. He was no longer just a horse whose heart was broken when his human set him free and left with a faceful of tears. He was much more.

Nero was something wilder than ever before, his soul not restrained to the Earthen plane. With the thinning veil during this time of chaos, he could step through it into Hell and back to the Earthen plane. It did wonders for him hiding from Shay and Jed. He was a horse but he knew he wasn't supposed to be following them. Horses aren't dumb. And Nero was the smartest horse humanity had ever come across. Quite possibly, the most dangerous.

Chapter 33

Shay had never been kissed like this before. Jed's lips were firm, searching, his tongue demanding. Need grew in Shay's belly. Her fingers pressed into Jed's shoulders before sliding across smooth muscle exploring the dips and valleys of his body before delving up into his hair.

Jed's hands gripped her hips and pulled her down against him with a deep groan.

"We have to go," Shay said, out of breath, cheeks flushed and lips swollen.

"Where?" Jed buried his face in her chest, leaving wet marks from his dripping hair.

"California. We'll be two days behind if we stay another night here."

"Fuck California." Jed didn't care. In this moment, he only cared about the current situation; Shay on his lap, the cold stream keeping him grounded. Not a care in the world.

Tree branches snapped. Jed moved fast, standing to shield Shay with his body and holding out his free hand ready to cast.

Nero broke through the bramble and dipped his head to drink from the stream.

Shay started to laugh. "Nero! Where have you been all night?" She weaved around Jed and moved toward the horse, petting him and resting her head on his side.

Nero was a cock-blocking horse if Jed ever saw one. While Shay was distracted, he finished cleaning himself and got his body under control, cursing himself for letting his guard down. This time it was the horse, next time it could be anything.

CHAPTER 34

JED AND SHAY DECIDED TO PACK UP AND HEAD OUT in the evening. The land Shay had found wasn't far from the road where she'd killed the Angel and Jed was worried more Angels would come looking for them.

Shay said goodbye to Nero and warned him to stay away from the walking corpses. One large dark eye was watching Jed as Shay whispered at the horse. She didn't feel as alone this time, not as overwhelmed by death or her own mortality. All this time she'd thought her family would keep her safe, she'd figured Nicholas and Momma would help her make it through these times of the dead walking and demons wrecking the ranch. Shay was wrong. She was strong enough to stay alive, strong enough to keep others alive. She'd killed a murderous Angel and saved Jed. She took a deep breath and focused.

This time, the goodbye wasn't as devastating. Nero galloped off toward the prairie and didn't chase the Jeep like last time. It was easier for both of them, not a goodbye but a promise to see each other again.

Shay rolled down the window and let the night air fill the Jeep. The vehicle jerked to the side.

Jed made a noise and held his ribs.

"Sorry," Shay said as she looked at him, "just a pot hole."

"It's all good." Jed was eating one of the freeze dried camp meals. Cheeseburger macaroni and a pack of space ice cream.

"You gonna eat all our food in one night, big guy?" Shay asked.

"Sorry." He chewed and swallowed. "It's just the healing," he motioned to his body, "thing I've got going on. I burn a lot of calories."

Shay bit her lip, thinking of another way to burn calories.

Jed stilled. "Don't," he warned like he could read her mind.

"You said fuck California earlier." Shay tipped a shoulder.

"We have to go if we're going to make it out of this mess alive."

Shay gripped the steering wheel and focused straight ahead. She was the planning type and an adventure like this was sure to go sideways real quick without a strategy. "So we get to California and then what?"

Jed finished chewing a spoonful of cheeseburger mac. "We get to California and get ahead of the horde."

"A horde of the dead?"

"Yes."

"Won't they kill us?"

Jed waved the spoon. "Not necessarily. We come down

from the North and find Sparrow first. Then we should be fine."

"*Should be*." Shay wasn't sure she had enough bullets in her pack for *should be*.

Jed nodded. "The horde is following him. They won't get too close to him."

"How do you know?" Shay couldn't hide the concern in her voice. She'd done things these past few days that she never thought she'd do. She watched her family die. She'd killed an Angel. She was very much enjoying the man sitting next to her in the Jeep. She didn't want it all to end being torn apart by a horde of the walking dead.

"I know because I tattooed him with Meg's blood. Runes like mine to hide him from Angels and Demons."

"The same Meg who bit your neck?"

"Same one."

"Why did he need to be hidden?"

"He's been through some things. He was a prince of the Seven Kingdoms of Heaven. Then the Legion Commander of Hell. Meg's Legion Commander. But she stabbed him in the heart and released the last spec of his angel grace. He is darkness now, an enigma walking the Earthen plane. Darkness follows darkness."

"This sounds bad."

"It could be. But I don't think it will be. The horde is following something. It has to be him."

"So we find him and we have protection?" Shay asked.

"Until we get him back to Meg. They are supposed to be together. Or at least, that's what they're always saying to each other."

"Like a forbidden love kind of thing."

"Destiny. Maybe." Jed ate more, scraping the bag until every drop was gone.

"You believe in destiny?" Shay asked.

"I believed that I wasn't safe to be around. That anyone I loved would die if they were around me. I believed that I was meant for a solitary life. Then I met you." Jed was staring, he couldn't help it. "Something led us to meet. It had to be destiny."

"Maybe luck?"

"I do have considerable luck." Jed smiled as he tore open the pack of freeze-dried ice cream. "Chocolate?"

Shay nodded and he broke off a piece and held it to her mouth.

Shay's lips touched his fingertips.

Jed made a noise deep in his throat. "This is going to be a long ride."

CHAPTER 35

THE THING IS, WHEN YOU MAKE A DEAL WITH A crossroads Demon, you're rarely ever allowed to die and stay dead. Clyburn was dragged down into that hole the four Demons climbed out of at the ranch. He'd promised his soul to Hell and Hell was going to collect. Souls were important; they gave power to whomever sat on the throne. A deal became a transfer of souls upon death. When the crossroads Demon died by Jed's hand, Clyburn took its place. There had to be balance, after all.

Clyburn's corpse twitched and jerked and after his heart started beating again, he took a few breaths. His eyes flashed open. He was no longer on the Dunn ranch, he was near it. A thinning veil was the only obstacle. Clyburn's hand broke through the soil outside the gates of the ranch and he crawled out of the ground with purpose.

"Out of the eater will come something to eat. And out of the strong will come something sweet." Clyburn smiled and held out a dusky hand with long necrotic fingernails. One thing was missing: the golden ring and bracelet of the

Crossroads Demon. "My precious," Clyburn said, anger and hunger in his black eyes.

Clyburn sniffed the air. There was no one alive at the ranch. Everything was dead. Clyburn licked his lips as he turned toward the road. He sniffed again, smelled the trace of Shay that was fading fast.

Clyburn took to the road, dropping down to all fours like a bloodhound on the hunt, his elbows and knees bent awkwardly. He ran after Shay's trail.

-The End-

About the Author

M. R. Pritchard, a captivating author, delves into the profound clash between good and evil, the mystical realms of gods and monsters, and the intricate transformations of ordinary people into beings of immense power. Her gripping narratives often unfold within the haunting backdrop of apocalyptic or post-apocalyptic landscapes, offering a unique blend of suspense and wonder.

M. R. Pritchard is a two-time Kindle Scout winning author, her short story "Glitch" has been featured in the 2017 winter edition of THE FIRST LINE literary journal. Her short story "Moon Lord" has been featured in Chronicle Worlds: Half Way Home (Part of the Future Chronicles) and will be time capsuled on the moon on the Lunar Codex in 2024. M. R. Pritchard holds degrees in Biochemistry and Nursing. She is a northern New Yorker transplanted to the Gulf Coast of Florida who enjoys coffee, mint chocolate, cloudy days, and reading on the lanai.

Visit her website MRPritchard.com and Subscribe for free. You'll get subscriber only content, updates, special previews of new projects, and book deals.

———

Other Books by M. R. Pritchard

Science Fiction/post-apocalyptic:
The Phoenix Project
The Reformation
Revelation
Inception
Origins
Resurrection
The Phoenix Project Compendium Edition
The Safest City on Earth
The Man Who Fell to Earth
Heartbeat

Asteroid Riders Series
Moon Lord
Collector of Space Junk and Rebellious Dreams

Steampunk:
Tick of a Clockwork Heart

Dark Fantasy:
Sparrow Man Series/Veil of Shadows Series
Sparrow Man
Nightingale Girl
Scarecrow
Raven King
Nightjar
Night Owl
Etched in Darkness

Thread the Bone

Preview of "Embrace the Night" [UNEDITED]

Chapter 1

Shay wasn't one to believe in ghosts but she couldn't shake the feeling that someone was watching her.

Gooseflesh rose on her arms and the back of her neck and it wasn't from the water she was washing in. Jed wasn't far away, he rarely was, but Shay took some time for privacy by the cold mountain stream. She didn't want to call out to him like a fearful child. From her periphery she saw a figure in white, wavering. Just for a moment then it was gone. She told herself it was nothing and she turned, expecting to see someone but saw Nero step onto the riverbank.

"Hey, boy," Shay wrapped herself in a blanket and walked toward the black stallion. "It's been a while." Shay stroked Nero's face.

They hadn't seen Nero since the last night they'd spent in Montana while Jed healed up enough to travel. It had been a few days since then. Jed and Shay had traveled through most of Idaho, sticking close to the National Forests where rest stops and stores were present but the population wasn't. They'd driven past Boise National Forest at midnight and avoided most of the dead wandering out of the towns and cities. Jed had been correct, the dead were headed west, toward California. They'd seen the dead moving in herds like a cattle drive without a cowboy. The largest of the zombie horde wasn't far from Fort Bragg. Jed had a plan to travel south and not get too close, intercepting Sparrow before it got too dangerous.

Jed and Shay were making their way through a portion of Oregon that was mostly uninhabited, there wasn't much to see besides foothills and the prairies and the mountains in the distance. It was scenic at least. The backdrop to their travels didn't force one to dwell on the fact that the dead were walking and biting.

Shay was surprised she didn't see Nero as they drove. She figured, being a horse and all, that he'd found some other route. Maybe one with some wild horses so he wasn't lonely. It's all Shay could hope for her beloved friend.

"I miss you," Shay said as she stroked Nero's flank and noticed how shiny his coat had become now that he was living free. She hoped he'd found happiness in the fresh air and open fields and had recovered from what they'd endured at the ranch in Montana.

Nero huffed and rubbed his head against her shoulder before drinking from the stream.

Shay dressed in clean clothes then gathered her belongings. She paused, finding a small ring with a blue stone tucked between the rocks at the bank of the stream. These days, money was no good mist places but a ring could be a wager. Shay tucked it in her pocket, then went to find Jed.

"Don't be a stranger," she told Nero with the wave of her hand.

CHAPTER 2

Clyburn followed the fading scent of Shay across the Montana foothills. He didn't care to hide his hideous form of a man running on all fours, elbows and knees bent at awkward angles. His claws tapped on the crumbling asphalt of the road. He leapt over broken down cars, agile as a panther. Being a Crossroads Demon, Clyburn was nothing more than a shadow in the periphery to a human on the Earthen plane, one moment he was there, the next he was a figment of their imagination. An errant shadow of a bird flying overhead, the whisper of a heavy tree branch in the wind. Nothing, apparently. Clyburn moved swiftly with ease through the Earthen plane, undisturbed since the balance was off. The Veil separating the realms was thinner than ever now that a Hellion walked the Earthen plane.

Clyburn stopped in the road, sniffed the pile of ashes that were once a punishing Angel. There was a drop of Shay's blood. Clyburn licked it off the asphalt, tilted his nose to the sky and sniffed. She'd backtracked. Clyburn went off running, fueled by the drop of Shay's blood, he ran faster.

Stopping at a fork in the road, Clyburn smelled Shay in

both directions. Humans were creatures of habit. And Shay-baby knew where she belonged, on the ranch. Clyburn figured she changed her mind, left that abomination Jed and went home.

He wanted her. He wanted the shiny dangle of the Crossroads Demon ring and bracelet. The old gold was ancient, power filled, his. He'd kill Jed for taking it. He'd kill Jed for taking Shay.

"Precious," Clyburn grumbled as he missed the feel of it on his wrist even though he'd never touched it before ascending. Jed had cut it off the previous Demon and ran off with it. It belonged on Clyburn's hand. It was *his*.

He leapt over fallen trees two at a time and veered into the forests of the foothills to hide his shadow from the sunlight that broke the cloud cover. He slid under the chain that crossed a hidden driveway and slowed his pace.

Clyburn prowled, hunted. He stuck to the shadows as he walked down the driveway. He wanted to surprise them, shock them, he wanted to consume them. The crossbreed abomination would be first. Clyburn licked his lips, imagining the taste of sweet meat, imagining the crunch of magic filled bones. Yes, he would eat Jed first. But Shay, she would be a treat to be savored. She would display nicely at his hovel in Hell. He thought about the chains he could lock her in, the table he could strap her to. His filthy body hardened at thoughts of Shay at his mercy. He'd had thoughts of her like that since the moment he met her at that dive bar near Colstrip. She was easy, innocent, and followed his lead that night. Then she played hard to get. Clyburn knew better. He knew she craved his hard body just as he craved her softness. He'd make her see. He'd show her. Shay was his.

Clyburn stopped, dropped low to the ground, and watched the clearing ahead of him. There was a shack but nothing more. Fresh tire tracks in the dirt driveway led Clyburn to believe that they had been there. He walked closer, unafraid. Her scent was strong and it let him to a tree ncar a bubbling stream. Strips of cloth hung from a branch. Clyburn ripped them down and smelled them. Jed's scent was strong but Shay's was there. He examined the stream and tire tracks under the tree. They'd been there then left.

Clyburn cursed himself for assuming she'd gone home. He took the wrong path where the road bisected. She wasn't going home, she was still leaving.

Clyburn snarled and roared. He dug his claws into the dirt, using purchase in the soil as a launching pad and took off.

Chapter 3

"Do you believe in ghosts?" Shay asked Jed as he drove a winding, empty road.

Jed gave her a hard look. "Ghosts are rarely ghosts." He bit the inside of his cheek, preparing himself for what she was about to say. He'd warned her to tell him when she saw something strange. She was new to his world. Things that'd seemed normal rarely were. They held a deeper meaning, sometimes a darker meaning or message that something was coming.

"What did you see?" he asked.

Shay thumbed behind them. "Back at that stream I thought I saw a white figure. But then Nero was there."

"Did it say anything?" Jed asked.

"Not that I heard."

"How long did you see it for?"

"Just a second. I think." Shay rubbed her arms, remembering the feeling of being watched as she bathed.

Jed tapped his fingers on the steering wheel and chose his next words carefully. He didn't want to scare Shay. She'd probably punch him in the throat if he ever appeared threatening. He still had thoughts of her stabbing that Angel in the chest and killing him. Jed never wanted her to turn that wrath on him. He took a cleansing breath and slowed the Jeep so he could look at her.

"One second is enough to bring death to us both." Jed touched her hand. "If it happens again, I need to know right then."

Order your copy of "Embrace the Night" today!